'A finely drawn confluence of wa
concrete realities of the Cold War era. With her trademark elegant, teasing prose and some lumiously visionary writing, it is a satisfyingly slow-burn delight, in the tradition of Susan Hill and M. R. James.'

Kate Worsley, author of *She Rises* (Winner of the HWA Debut Crown for Historical Fiction) and *Foxash*'

'*Lines and Shadows* is a rich beauty of a novella - part love story, part thriller, with an undertow of the uncanny.'

Heather Richardson, author of *A Dress for Kathleen*

'A gripping, unsettling novel, where nothing is quite what it seems. Bower's Suffolk is a wild and unforgiving place at the very edge of the Cold War, where everything might be swept away in a moment.'

Guinevere Glasfurd, Costa shortlisted author

# Also by Sarah Bower

The Needle in the Blood
The Book of Love
Erosion (writing as S. A. Hemmings)

# Lines and Shadows

Sarah Bower

**Story Machine**

*Lines and Shadows*, copyright © Sarah Bower, 2023

Print ISBN: 9781912665273
Ebook ISBN: 9781912665280
Published by Story Machine
130 Silver Road, Norwich, NR3 4TG;
www.storymachines.co.uk

Sarah Bower has asserted her right under Section 77 of the Copyright, Designs and Patents Act 1988 to be identified as the author of this work.

Set in Garamond.

Printed and bound in the UK by Seacourt Ltd.

Story Machine is committed to planet positive publishing. Our world is better off for every single book we print.

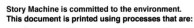

Story Machine is committed to the environment.
This document is printed using processes that are:

Printed by **seacourt** – proud to be counted amongst the top environmental printers in the world

# Lines and Shadows

Sarah Bower

For my sister, Jenny Gorvin, and all the others alongside whom
I lived through (and failed to remember) The Sixties

# 1

The stiff envelope had the hue of clotted cream against the pale green everyday Poole pottery. The Ministry of Defence seal gleamed like anthracite. Ginny's father had his Daily Mail up to his face as usual, in a way which somehow created the optical illusion that it was the paper eating his toast rather than him. Her mother fussed unnecessarily with the kettle, hummed, turned up the Home Service News, turned it down again. Ginny set the envelope aside, lifted the cosy off her egg cup and began to slice the top off her egg.

'Well,' said her mother eventually, 'aren't you going to open it?' Ginny's mother wasn't patient; pressure built up in her as if she were a small, volatile volcano and had to find instant release.

'In a minute, mum.' Ginny wasn't being unkind, but she hadn't expected the letter to arrive so soon and she needed a few minutes to make herself ready for whatever it might have to say. She was more like her dad, she supposed, whose rhythmic biting and chewing had suffered no interruption, although she did notice a slight tremor running through the front page, making Mr. MacMillan's moustache twitch. She stared into her egg, assessing the thickness of the white and the number of degrees off a circle of the circumference of the yoke. She didn't exactly know she was doing this, just that the progress of the calculations through her mind calmed her so her hands were hardly shaking at all when she picked up the letter and opened it.

It was a short letter, and she read it twice before saying anything, just to be absolutely certain she hadn't made a mistake. She hadn't.

'I got it,' she said quietly. 'I got the job.'

## 2

As her train steamed eastwards the rain gave way to a quilt of white cloud, cities to small, poor-looking hamlets, the Pennine crags to the Lincolnshire Wolds to a landscape so flat you could almost imagine God's hand smoothing it the way her mother smoothed a bedspread. If you believed in God. The previous summer, Ginny had graduated from the Manchester College of Science and Technology with a first class honours degree in applied mathematics and she knew perfectly well the flatness of the land was to do with the measurable density of rock, with wind speeds and the work of gravity upon water. There was no mystery, merely that which had yet to be discovered.

She disliked the countryside. All of it. When she was two, she and her mother had been evacuated to a village in Wales where everything smelt of dung and damp plaster and her mother, who was expecting her brother, Joe, cried as endlessly as it rained outside so she came to believe her

dad was actually dead. She was five when he came to collect them at the end of the war, and she ran away because
she was sure he was an escaped POW come to murder
them. She'd been hoping so much for a posting in London,
or Cyprus or Germany, any of those places mentioned on
Two Way Family Favourites. If she'd been to a proper university, she would probably have got one, but she had had
to make do, her father explained, because they needed to
save money for Joe's future. A boy had to have a proper
future. So she had to content herself with the college, and a
degree awarded by the Victoria University up the nice end
of Oxford Road, and was posted to Aldeford. It had taken
her some time to find it on a map.

After changing at Birmingham and Ipswich, the final
leg of her journey took her on a two-carriage train full of
Easter holidaymakers to Felixstowe. She had to share her
compartment with a gang of tipsy Teddy Boys and was sure
she must reek of beer and Brylcreem by the time she
dragged her case on to the platform at Felixstowe where
she had been told a car would meet her. Dusk was falling
and she hunted in vain among the throng on the station
forecourt for anyone who looked as if they might have
come from Aldeford Air Force Base. She failed to spot a
scrap of RAF blue among the optimistic summer colours
of her fellow travellers. As the station emptied and darkness deepened, she became certain she had been forgotten.
Had she got the date of travel wrong? Not possible. The
MoD had sent her tickets. Well, she thought, if it came to it
she could always take a taxi; the local cabbies must be familiar with the base. She just hoped it wasn't too far and
she would have enough money to cover her fare.

'Are you the new computer? I was expecting a guy but
you seem to be all that's left. I thought it was…intriguing
they'd got us rooming together.' The voice was a sophisti-

cated-sounding drawl, a hybrid of American and upper-class English, the girl to whom it belonged an even more surprising encounter in an old-fashioned English seaside town. Despite the fact that it was almost dark, she wore oversize sunglasses with tortoiseshell frames, a boilersuit cinched tight at the waist with a heavy leather belt and workmen's boots. Her flame red hair was bound up landgirl style in an expensive-looking silk scarf. She held out a hand and Ginny took it; she had a firm, boyish grip and bright scarlet nails.

'Yes,' said Ginny eventually, 'I suppose I am.' The girl responded with a decidedly unladylike whistle between her teeth; she was wearing, Ginny noticed, the sort of lipstick her mother would describe as 'tarty', a dusk-defying match for her nails. 'You're a first, then. God knows what they'll make of you on the Island. I'm Frank, by the way.'

'Virginia Matlock. Ginny.'

'Ah, so that's what the "V" stands for. I'd decided you were Vincent.' Frank picked up Ginny's suitcase and swung it effortlessly as she led the way to an American jeep, flamboyantly parked with one wheel up on the kerb and its rear end stuck out half way across the road. 'Climb in,' she said, flinging the suitcase into a well behind the seats. In her straight skirt, Ginny couldn't emulate Frank and leap into the jeep without opening the door, and felt Frank's gaze upon her as she settled herself primly, feet and knees together, hands folded over her handbag in her lap. Frank made her uncomfortable; her scrutiny was too intent, too – well – frank. And they were to share a room? She was glad when the other girl turned her attention to the road and Ginny could try to set her impressions in order. She had more questions than answers but for now it was a relief to have nothing more to concentrate on than not being thrown out of the vehicle as it rattled and lurched along potholed lanes with high hedgerows looming either side. She tried not to think about what would happen if they encountered anything coming the other way. She wished Frank would remove the dark glasses.

The hedgerows gave way to dunes, strange sculpted shapes that glimmered palely into view and were gone as the headlights passed over them. Frank made an abrupt right turn and, after a few hundred yards, halted the jeep in the middle of an unlit space whose borders were vaguely demarcated by the silhouettes of buildings and buttery squares and oblongs of lit windows. From the largest of these spilled voices and piano music as well as light, and a sign above it proclaimed The Merman Inn. An unusual name, Ginny thought.

'Here we are,' said Frank. The jeep was the only motor vehicle parked in the square, whose surface was beaten earth rather than tarmac, though a horse and cart were tethered outside the pub. Frank heaved Ginny's suitcase out of the jeep and set off past the pub, which stood at one corner of the square. The dimly illuminated sign displayed a crude and shocking image of the merman, suspended by his tail over a fire basket, curls of hair and fire entwined in the sign painter's fancy.

Momentarily distracted by the pub sign, Ginny had to move smartly to catch up with Frank's long, swinging stride. As they rounded the end of the pub, the ground sloped away and Ginny found herself in a narrow lane, bordered on one side by a row of terraced cottages and on the other by a ruined tower. Entirely in darkness, it formed a dense, crenellated silhouette against a sky which now shimmered with wintry starlight. A chilly breeze had got up, bearing the scent of salt and seaweed, rustling the ivy which shrouded the tower. Ginny shivered; she hoped there wasn't much further to go. You'll be making a vital contribution to our Cold War effort, Brigadier Bough-Mantle had told her at her interview, absolutely essential work to keep the country safe. In the godforsaken wilds of Suffolk, on a cold spring night of knifing, ghostly wind, she felt utterly unequal to the task, unequal to anything, in fact, other than a hot bath, a mug of cocoa and a night's sleep.

'I won't be living on the base, then?' she asked, as Frank stopped in front of a cottage, rummaging in one of her voluminous pockets for a key which she thrust into the lock of a Brunswick green-painted door. A matching boot scraper sat to one side of it and on the other a plant pot containing a very dead geranium.

'Oh no, only the military live on the base, the rest of us are billeted in the village. You'll be sharing with me and Alicia. This is home. Briar Cottage. Alicia's the sleeping beauty.' She laughed, opened the door and stood aside to let Ginny enter.

The door opened straight on to a shabby front parlour, the walls a nicotine beige in the patchy light from a standard lamp in one corner and an Anglepoise with a broken arm spring which lolled drunkenly over the edge of a deal table with four rush-bottomed chairs tucked under it. A lugubrious sideboard stood beneath the window to the right of the door, and next to it a treadle sewing machine. A sagging sofa upholstered in dark brown chenille and an armchair of indeterminate hue made up the rest of the room's furnishings. It was at least warm, with a log fire crackling in a tiled fireplace. The rug in front of it, Ginny noticed, was blotched with scorch marks. The only object in the room which did not share the signs of long and impersonal use was a smart red and cream portable Dansette balanced on top of a crate full of records in the space under the stairs.

Framed in the open doorway to the kitchen, from

which clouds of steam and a smell of boiled potatoes emanated, was a remarkably tall, willowy girl wearing a blue silk kimono over a pair of denim cigarette pants and a white teeshirt. Large, lilac-grey eyes looked out from beneath strong brows and a tangle of loose, dark curls. Until she smiled, she had a mouth like a Victoria plum but when she smiled everything below her nose was large white teeth.

'I cooked,' she announced, in an accent which went with the aristocratic nose but was at odds with the wide and enthusiastic smile. 'Sausage and mash.'

'Hunky dory,' said Frank. 'This is Ginny. Ginny, Alicia.' Alicia stepped forward and offered Ginny a long, pale hand to shake. Her nails were bitten to the quick.

'So, you're a computer. How exciting. We haven't had a girl computer before, have we, darling?'

'Sure ain't,' said Frank. Ginny wondered if the Brunswick green door were some kind of time machine and she had stepped back into the 1940s.

'It's 1960,' she said, cursing herself for sounding defensive. 'There have been women computers in America for ten years. Grace Hopper? Katherine Johnson?' The other girls looked blank, then Frank said,

'Best thing to come out of America, apart from me, of course…'

'But you're only half American.' Alicia gave Frank's shoulder a playful push.

'…apart from me, is Otis Redding.'

'Ignore her, Ginny. We're in awe of you, really. You must be so clever.'

'Well, I don't know who Otis Redding is.' She wanted to be conciliatory. She was tired of being the odd one out, an object of wary curiosity like a walrus in the Thames or a woman in Parliament. Yet the looks turned on her by her new housemates made it immediately clear she had only made things worse. Dumping Ginny's case unceremoniously beside the front door, Frank crossed to the Dansette, slipped a single out of the stack of records and put it on the turntable.

It was a live recording, the music emerging from a chaos of voices as if being played in a crowded bar, like a scene, Ginny thought, from one of those black and white musicals her mother loved on Sunday afternoon television. The impossible moment when everything magically came together and parallels converged, and now there was a tight blare of horns, a bass guitar picking out a rhythm, a voice full of raw energy and Frank singing along with it and dancing slick -hipped around the dull little room, her scarlet nails flashing as she moved in and out of the light.

'That's Otis Redding,' she breathed as the song ended, her green eyes dancing like birch leaves in a wind. 'That's what we're saving the world for.' Only when she heard the percussion of pots and pans from the kitchen did Ginny realise Alicia was no longer in the doorway.

Returning from wherever the music had taken her, Frank gave herself a little shake and found an LP of something cooler, more jazz-lounge, to play while Alicia served up the sausage and mash and tinned peas on a set of mismatched plates. To the spun-out wail of a saxophone, Alicia explained that she and Frank were secretaries: she to the base commander, Wing Commander Drummond, and Frank to the American Air Force liaison office. So all they could really tell Ginny with any certainty was that civilian staff travelled to the base and back on a flotilla of small boats. As Ginny didn't know, or couldn't tell them, where she would be working, they could say no more.

'I would,' Ginny assured them. ''I assume we've all signed the Official Secrets Act.'

'There are still different clearances, though,' said Frank.

'Are there? I had no idea.'

'I guess that means you've signed the whole thing. Top level clearance.' Their eyes, the green and the lilac, fixed on her, Alicia's amazed, Frank's impossible to read. To Ginny, bone-tired as she was after her long journey, in the fug of the warm sitting room with a full stomach, their combined gaze felt like a weight leaning on her. It took an effort of will to get up from her chair, stack the plates and carry them to the kitchen. She must show willing with the household chores, yet if she sat there much longer, she would drop into an abyss of sleep.

'There are tinned peaches,' said Alicia, 'and condensed milk.'

'That's so kind, but I'm exhausted, I'm afraid. Can I save mine till tomorrow?'

'Of course. Frankie, take note.'

'I promise to keep watch for the phantom peach snatcher and fight him off with my trusty can opener.'

'Hypocrite.' Alicia threw her napkin at Frank. Removing it from her shoulder and throwing it back, Frank said,

'Your room is the one at the front, right at the top of the stairs. The bathroom leads straight off the kitchen, I'm afraid. No idea of bathrooms when this place was built.' Ginny had assumed that to be the case; they had lived in a similar house until she was eight and her father earned the promotion that enabled them to move to the villa in Didsbury where her parents lived now.

'So quaint,' added Alicia, 'though we do keep chamber pots upstairs. Horrible having to traipse down in the middle of a cold night.' Yes, thought Ginny, yes, it was, but a step up from the lean to in the back yard, the spiders, the mildewed copies of the London Illustrated News.

'And sorry about the bikes,' called Frank as Ginny was putting the plates in the kitchen sink. 'We used to keep them under the stairs before the Dansette arrived.'

She used the bathroom, where three bicycles served as tolerable towel rails, then dragged her case up the steep, narrow stairs, across a cramped landing to her room. In contrast to the sitting room, the air was gelid, thick with a must of damp and mothballs. She wondered how long it was since anyone had slept in it. Yet the bed was made up, with a jaunty coverlet of crocheted squares, and there were towels folded on the end of it which exhaled a thin breath of lavender when she picked them up. Something told her this was Alicia's work. The dressing table drawers were neatly lined with offcuts of a floral wallpaper and the chamber pot beneath the bed, though it had a chip in its rim, was flawlessly clean and smelled of Jeyes Fluid. She unlaced her shoes and crossed the room in her stockinged feet to draw the curtains, the carpet rough and threadbare beneath her tread.

Even in the darkness, she could appreciate how a view of the tower filled her bedroom window. Crumbling atop its mound it loomed over the row of cottages, once, perhaps, reassuring to the villagers it was built to protect, but tonight it seemed to Ginny like a cold breath from a past riddled with violence and superstition. Yet at least she did not have to overlook the pub, with its macabre sign. Her hand on the edge of the curtain was stayed by movement, bats, perhaps, or an owl, or the sheep which grazed on the mound.

'It's just a sheep lavatory nowadays,' Frank had said as they walked past the tower earlier. Ginny whisked the curtain shut and set about lighting the Calor gas heater that stood in front of the room's small fireplace, to take the edge off the cold before climbing under the covers.

# 3

She knew no more until her travelling alarm clock was ringing in her ear and Frank's voice on the other side of her door was confirming that it was six a.m. The light filtering through the curtains promised a fine morning. She opened them on to a cloudless sky, an expanse of delicate aquamarine behind the castle, shading to primrose yellow as she looked to her left, to the east and the sea and the rising sun. The light gilded the tower's old stones, lending them a honey-eyed glow and haloing the sheep as they cropped the mound. In daylight she could see the tower was only part of the ruin, that an arch at its base gave on to a courtyard surrounded by the rubble of walls. A pair of gulls perched on the battlements, their morning quarrel easily loud enough to be heard through the glass; they rose into the air as a horse-drawn milk float clopped past then returned to their perch and continued their squabble. The sea itself was barely a glint in the corner of Ginny's eye yet it pervaded everything, as if the light only came to her refracted from its surface.

As the girls walked down the lane after breakfast, it dipped completely out of sight of the water, but the sea's restless shushing filled Ginny's ears and she could taste salt on her tongue. Her lungs filled with the iodine tang of sea-weed. Outside the final cottage in the row they were joined by two other girls, one introduced as Jean, the other whose name she failed to catch. Jean, who was short and curva-ceous and wearing a pink bobble hat, cast Ginny a mourn-ful look and asked,

'I suppose you're in poor Sue's room?'

'Sue?' Custodian, she assumed, of the third bicycle in the bathroom.

'Yes. Surely they've told you…'

'Those are our boats.' The lane had opened out on to a broad sandy space strewn with fishing boats and tractors. There was a slipway into a narrow channel of steely water and a row of mooring posts alongside it. A single storey building of gunmetal grey weatherboarding with a lookout tower bore a sign beside the door proclaiming it to be the harbourmaster's office. Flags and a windsock snapped from the pole on its roof. The boats to which Frank was point-ing were moored together, six of them, painted in matching camouflage with outboard motors and cross thwarts and a uniformed helmsman sitting in the stern of each. Ginny had no time to wonder about the mysterious 'poor Sue' as the civilians employed on the base converged on the boats and jostled for places. There were ten of them to each boat. She found herself sitting between Alicia and a nondescript man of indeterminate age who reminded her of the clerks in her father's office, kindly, balding, with pockets full of humbugs. Men in whose eyes she would never be more than ten or eleven, an odd little girl with an arithmetic book in the corner of the room. Alicia turned round to chat to the girls sitting behind her, the man fought with the breeze for his newspaper as their boat bobbed out into the channel.

The channel was not wide, but the breeze blowing straight across their bow from the south made it choppy. Ginny enjoyed a day on the beach as much as the next person but she was wary of the sea. Its endless, restless shifting made it feel to her like a bad night's sleep interrupted by dreams of impermanence. She checked her appointment letter was safe in her handbag and checked again, and then their helmsman was throttling back the motor as they came alongside the base landing stage. As she watched his manoeuvres, something unexpected appeared in the tail of her eye, something dark and round, there and then gone.

'What was that?' The words seemed to well up involuntarily from somewhere deep in her unconscious, prompted by an instinctive fear of the unknown, the unexpected.

'What was what?' asked Frank, turning to face Ginny from the thwart in front, the breeze kindling the flames of her hair.

'I don't know. It looked like a…a…head. Floating in the water. Should we report it? Call out the coastguard or something?'

'My, darling,' Alicia exclaimed, 'you're as white as a sheet! I expect it was a seal. There's a big colony at Walberswick, not so far from here. Sometimes they even come up on the Island. I think they like watching us.' Alicia squeezed her hand, an intimacy which made Ginny feel all the more foolish and disconcerted. She forced a laugh as the helmsman leapt out of the boat to secure it to the landing stage.

Aldeford Island was, in fact, a long spit of sand still joined to the mainland five miles north of the base. Until some three hundred years earlier Aldeford had had a decent deep water harbour and was a prosperous port, exporting raw East Anglian wool to Flanders and bringing back finished Flemish weave for the burghers of Lowestoft and Norwich. But this was a shifting, friable coastline, its winds and tides sometimes throwing up great mounds and ridges of mud and sand to confound the dredgers that worked ceaselessly to keep the harbour clear, sometimes gnawing at the edges of the land, flooding dykes, turning marsh water brackish, sucking houses and byres and cattle into the sea. The Island was barely a few feet above sea level, knit together by the shallow roots of marram grass and sea thrift, held in place by a weighted hem of shingle and pebbles. Even on a morning such as this, when, now the sun was up, the light possessed the solidity of an impasto, the Island had a quality of shifting, dream-like impermanence. You felt as if it would take no more than a winter storm to blow it all away, the Nissen huts, the blockhouses, the radio masts, the smartly snapping flags, the landing stage and the bobbing boats, empty now as the workers followed paths marked out by white-painted boulders towards their offices and laboratories.

Ginny accompanied Alicia to Wing Commander Drummond's office, her cheeks still burning from her foolishness over the seal, her heart thudding in her chest as if she had just run a race. What would her work here be? All her letter of appointment said was that she had been posted to 'general computing duties' at RAF Aldeford. It could mean anything she thought despairingly, as she followed Alicia along a sandy path towards a two-storey weatherboard block painted Air Force blue with a flagpole outside it, surrounded neatly by the ubiquitous white marker stones. Her contribution to the Cold War effort might just as easily be accounting for supplies as calculating missile trajectories.

'You'll be joining Section Four,' the Wing Commander

told her, after they had exchanged pleasantries about her journey from Manchester, her accommodation, and the idiosyncrasies of the Island. He was a bluff, avuncular figure with a network of broken veins over the bridge of his nose that spoke of an enjoyment of a drink. His eyes, however, had a cool, grey distance to them that left her in no doubt that he could give the order to launch a nuclear missile without breaking a sweat, if called upon to do so. 'It's all men, of course. Bit of a poser where to put you to be honest, but I think you'll be comfortable there. Phin Mac-Namara, the chief engineer, is a married man and the photography analyst, Adrian Fletcher, is a bit older. Couple of kids, seven, eight, thereabouts. Just as well.' He left the last comment hanging and Ginny wondered what it was about Adrian Fletcher which made it just as well he had children. He cleared his throat. 'There are a few young chaps as well, of course, but Phin and Adrian will take care of you.'

'And the work?' she enquired.

'Ah yes. Triggers. Not the triggers themselves, you understand, we don't do that here. Boffins elsewhere. What Section Four is doing is designing bomb-proof housings for the triggers. I know you've signed the Official Secrets Act so I don't have to tell you that nothing you do can be discussed with anyone, not even your housemates. Neither of them has the same clearance level.' Nor, Ginny speculated, was it likely either of them would be very interested. Frank apparently thought only of American pop music and Alicia seemed to have no passions at all, wherever she was behind the screen of vague and generalised niceness which enveloped her. 'Decent girls at Briar Cottage. Such good fortune you came along when you did. Take their minds off poor Sue Reynolds.' And as if he knew she was about to ask about 'poor Sue' and did not want to have to give her an answer, he picked up the phone on his desk and spoke briefly into the receiver.

'Do come in, Bonn. Miss Matlock is ready to go to her section now.'

Flight Lieutenant Ralph Bonney – 'Call me Bonn, everyone does, like the city' – appeared every inch the flyboy with his chiselled jaw and a dark blond quiff which fell into his blue eyes and had to be scraped back under his cap whenever he put it on.

'Section Four's out on the edge,' he said as he led her towards the seaward side of the Island, 'I should think a girl computer will fit right in.'

'Can I ask you a question?'

'If the answer is eight o'clock in The Merman, ask away.'

Ginny shuddered, an image of the macabre pub sign staining her mind. 'I very much doubt it,' she said, with more vehemence than she had intended.

'I know what you mean,' said Bonn, apparently taking no offence. 'It does have a bit of an odd atmosphere.'

'Odd how? I haven't been in there yet. It's just…that horrible sign. Hardly designed to welcome people in, is it?'

'It refers to the legend of the Aldeford Merman.' They walked on, the cinder path skirting a shallow, reed-fringed lake. Small black and white birds on long pink legs fossicked among the reeds. 'Avocets,' said Bonn, pausing to watch them. 'Quite rare now, but no-one disturbs them here because it's off-limits to the public. Proper conundrum that, atomic weapons protecting birds. Apparently there's a toad nearing extinction as well, but I've never seen that.'

'Tell me about the merman,' Ginny urged, and Bonn started to walk again, leaving the lake behind and heading towards a ruined lighthouse tower which stuck up into the clear spring sky like a broken finger.

'Well,' said Bonn, 'they say that during the reign of

Henry II, some fishermen caught a merman in their nets. They brought him ashore and presented him to the commander of the garrison in the castle, a man called Odon de la Tête Rouge who wasn't, it seems, known for his patience. He was curious, though, and he questioned the merman at length. I suppose you would, wouldn't you?'

'I would want not to have been made a fool of.'

'Ah, the mathematician. If there isn't a proof for it, it isn't real.'

Ginny gave a defensive little shrug. 'It's served me well so far.'

'I don't know how much of a mathematician this Odon de la Tête Rouge was, but he seems to have been very sure the merman had a story to tell because, when he refused to speak, Odon had him tortured. He chained him up by his tail in the dungeon and dangled him over a brazier till his hair caught fire, and even then, he said nothing.'

'And that, I suppose, is what the pub sign is all about.' Despite the mildness of the air she felt as if she were breathing in the dank chill of the castle dungeon.

'You get used to it,' said Bonn. 'I hardly notice it now, or the prints in the snug.'

'What happened to him? Did he die?'

'Amazingly not. The legend says Odon gave up and let him go, and the fishermen who'd caught him took him back out to sea. But – and this is the really odd part of the story – apparently he didn't leave. He swam about in the harbour for a couple of days, then came back ashore and disappeared.'

Ginny could find no response to this. The thought of the merman, unable to return to the sea yet unable to live among those whose touch had contaminated him, moved her inexplicably. Gödel's incompleteness theorems frightened her; the notion that, even in mathematics, statements existed which were neither provable nor refutable darkened the edges of her vision as though a storm were brewing just out of sight, over the wide, watery horizon. She did not trust herself to speak and they continued in silence until Bonn paused at the entrance to a low, broad building which looked like a small aircraft hangar.

'Well,' he said, 'here we are. Section Four. This is where I leave you. Until tonight?'

'You're very persistent, Flight Lieutenant.'

'I like the way you say that as if you mean it. You're not a flirt, are you?'

'I suppose not.' She was unsure whether she should feel flattered or insulted.

He smiled. 'I don't mean anything by it, just a welcome drink. Bring Frank and Alicia if you like.'

# 4

Inside Section Four, the space was sub-divided into an office and a larger area known as the Model Room where, she would come to learn, Phin MacNamara built maquettes of his designs. Phin's toys, the others called them. The floors were concrete, the walls corrugated iron, decorated, if that was the right word for it, with panels for soundproofing made out of cardboard egg cartons. Electric bar heaters created small bastions of warmth beneath the desks, though several of the pairs of eyes which looked up as Ginny and Bonn entered were framed by woollen hats and scarves and one man, no more than a boy really, with gangling limbs and a beaky nose which made him look like a heron, was also wearing fur ear muffs. Glass partitions and a door labelled 'P. MACNAMARA' separated one corner of the office from the rest. Beneath the printed sign some wag had Sellotaped a piece of paper on which was written, 'Chief Boffin and Bottlewasher'. Bonn knocked on the door then stepped smartly aside to allow Ginny to enter.

Phineas MacNamara was a small man, not much taller than Ginny herself, with sandy hair and green eyes and an accent you could chew. He hailed from Kerry, he told her, so liked his shoreline with a few more rocks, a bit more in the way of drama than this sandbar had to offer,

'But I'm here for the concrete,' he added, inviting her to sit and fussing with a kettle on a Primus stove in a corner behind his desk. 'I have, shall we say, an intimate relationship with concrete.'

Bonn laughed. 'He says that to all the girls. Strict instructions from Mrs. MacNamara.'

'Get away with you, Bonney, concrete is God and all His angels to me. Back with you to the Wing Commander. You know he can't find his hand to wipe his arse without you.'

'Ladies present, Phin, ladies present.'

'Ah, she'll hear a sight worse working in this place.' The kettle commenced a jig on top of the stove. 'Milk and sugar, Miss Matlock?'

'Yes please.' Her cheeks were burning; she hoped Mr. MacNamara would put it down to her having just come in out of the cold air.

Bonn left and she and Phin MacNamara settled with their tea either side of his desk, where a drift of papers was held in place beneath a large flint with a hole through the middle of it. Whatever his relationship with concrete, a wooden crucifix hung from the wall behind him.

'So, Miss Matlock,' he took a sip of tea, grimaced and said, 'I don't know where the MoD gets this stuff. A furniture factory floor maybe? Yes, now, Miss Matlock…'

'Ginny, please.'

'Ginny. And I'm Phin, with a ph.' It pleased Ginny that he made that clear, that he understood the importance of details. He gave a succinct account of Section Four's work, almost as though his body had been inhabited by a man quite other from the one whose desk was so untidy he ended up putting his undrunk mug of tea down on the floor. When the original man returned, Ginny knew he was going to kick the mug over the minute he stood up. But in explaining the task of calculating missile trajectories, blast impacts and the load-bearing capabilities of his beloved reinforced concrete he was meticulous. By the time he had kicked over the tea, fussed over it ineffectually with a tea towel, and taken Ginny out to introduce her to her colleagues in the main office, it didn't occur to her to question the rationality of creating bomb shelters for bombs.

Ginny's role, along with that of three young Cambridge graduates whose horn-rimmed glasses, varsity scarves and corduroy slacks seemed entirely interchangeable and who seemed to answer to any of the three names they were known by – Richard, Harry and Bill – was to 'crunch numbers' for Phin and his two technical draughtsmen, David (he of the fur ear muffs), and a nervous, pimply boy who refused to give his first name so was nicknamed Jonathan.

Their numbers were made up by Adrian, a quiet man in his forties, probably ten years older than Phin. Adrian had been an air reconnaissance photographer at the tail end of the war; his job now was to study photos taken of Hiroshima and Nagasaki during and after the American nuclear attacks and to convert what he saw into processable data for Ginny and RichardHarryBill. He had also been present when hydrogen bombs were tested on the Marshall Islands, but the reports and photographs from those had to be kept locked in his desk for security purposes. Only he and Phin had a high enough clearance to look at them. Although he seemed taciturn, a level-headed kindness emanated from him at which Ginny would come to marvel whenever she happened to pass his desk and catch sight of the things he was looking at.

Conversation in the office was limited in the main to only what was necessary to get the work done. It wasn't that the team was unfriendly, though Ginny did wonder if conversation had been freer before she arrived, but that the terrible acoustic, mitigated only a little by the egg carton panels, meant that even a loud sigh or the scratch of a pencil seemed to echo endlessly off the iron walls, the sound waves bouncing back and forth like tennis balls. Ginny could see them in her mind's eye, a grey web, and the eight of them as blithe as flies colliding with spiderwebs. She enjoyed the work, which stretched her, though always in directions which were already mapped on to her brain. Nevertheless, a sense of other questions, amorphous and difficult to grasp, lurked in the back of her mind like an impending fog and sometimes, unpredictably, distracted her.

She went to The Merman with Bonn that first night. She wanted to make friends here, to feel a part of this strange, hermetic world she had joined and to feel that she was not just a mathematical brain mistakenly encased in a female body. Perhaps, here, they would understand her and like her for herself. She had hoped Frank and Alicia would join her, but Alicia made a small, exasperated noise in the back of her throat and said she had to wash her hair, and Frank laughed.

'If at first you don't succeed,' she said. 'Go for it, Ginny. See if you can't exert your charms over our lovelorn Lieutenant Bonney. Alicia's broken his heart, you know.'

'Oh.' Ginny had blushed fiercely as her hopes dismantled themselves.

Thankfully, Bonn was enough of a gentleman not to

make his disappointment too obvious. He showed her to a corner table in the snug, where a good fire was lit and where he greeted several of the other customers whom she assumed also worked on the Island. As she waited for him to come back from the bar with her gin and French, she looked around at a series of prints hanging on the walls. Bonn had mentioned prints when they were talking about the merman earlier. Were these they? They seemed innocuous enough in the firelight, among the murmured conversations and sudden gusts of male laughter. The pub itself was welcoming, with limewashed stone walls, bright rugs on the flagged floor and a row of gleaming pumps along the bar. It was clean and well-kept and a long way from the spit and sawdust establishments her college friends back in Manchester had favoured.

She and Bonn chatted companionably enough, although it became clear quite quickly that they had nothing in common except the Island. He was good company, funny, attentive, relaxed and really quite handsome, until, emboldened by her drink, Ginny asked,

'So what did happen to my predecessor at the cottage? Sue Reynolds, was it? It sounds as if she left under something of a cloud.'

It was as if the air had turned suddenly colder. 'Someone should have told you,' he muttered, 'I'm not the right person.'

'Well, you seem to be the only person.' He turned to face her and she could see the conflicting demands of chivalry played out in the twist of his mouth, a whitening of the skin over the bridge of his nose. In the end he opted for the short, sharp shock.

'She drowned,' he said. He swallowed, his Adam's apple agitating in the open neck of his shirt. 'A bathing accident, just off the south of the island. Pretty fierce cross currents,' he added, as though trying to persuade himself of the truth of what he had said. He took a deep draft of his beer, then returned the glass to the table and stared into it.

'I'm sorry I put you through that,' said Ginny, 'Thank you for telling me. It must have been awful for you.' He was right. It shouldn't have been him, it should have been Drummond. Bonn went to buy another round. And her mind turned in upon itself, imagining the drowned girl in Briar Cottage. Eating at the battered deal table, washing up, dancing to Frank's records, mending the fire. Sleeping in the cold, bare room with the castle leaning against the window. She understood why her housemates hadn't said anything either.

The shadows cast by the fire seemed suddenly more threatening than cosy, animating the prints on the walls as they guttered in a draft blowing in under the door. Outside, she could hear the thin owl-screech of the pub sign hinges as it swung in the wind. She found herself getting up from her chair to examine the prints more closely. There were six of them, each etched in black and white and showing different episodes from the merman's grim tale, from a pair of muscular fishermen hauling the anguished creature aboard their boat to the creature lying on the beach, for all the world like a seal except for its human face, twisted in agony, fixed upon the sea to which it was condemned never to return. She thought of how, if you so much as touched a baby bird fallen from its nest, its parents would cease to recognise it and leave it to starve. Did he know from the outset, the poor, stranded creature, that those grasping human hands would bar him forever from his past? In pride of place over the bressumer beam above the fireplace was the same image as the pub sign: the creature hanging over the fire-basket, the serpent coils of his hair indistinguishable from the flames that licked among them.

Her scalp seemed to prickle with heat as she looked at it.

Grabbing her handbag, she hurried outside, just as Bonn was crossing the snug with their drinks. She couldn't stay there, she felt she could never enter that room again, with its hideous veneer of welcome and the horror beneath. The pulse in her temples pounded as she stood in the rising wind, the sign shrieking above her and an impression on her retinas of white faces turned towards her in consternation as she rushed out of the pub. Bonn followed her out.

'I'm sorry,' she said. 'I…I suddenly felt faint. I think I need to go home.' The word 'home' stuck in her throat. Briar Cottage wasn't home. How could she feel at home in the drowned girl's room, with the castle looming at the window and the merman crying in the wind? But where else could she go?

'I'll see you to your door,' said Bonn. In case you catch a glimpse of Alicia, Ginny thought bitterly.

'I'm alright, it's only a step, and it's out of your way.' Bonn had told her he lived on Quay Street, which led down to the sea from the opposite side of the square. She had set off before he could demur.

Time passed and no mention was made of Sue. Ginny understood their initial reluctance. That night, after Bonn had told her what had happened to Sue, she had stared with revulsion at the mattress which still held the shape of the dead girl's body, and considered asking Wing Commander Drummond if she could move to different digs. But she didn't want to be a troublemaker, and she was grateful to Drummond for giving her her job. He must, she supposed, have encountered a fair amount of opposition. She had settled for sleeping on the floor.

Perhaps, she speculated, girls of Frank and Alicia's class thought it ill-mannered to raise the fact that the girl who had occupied the room before her had died in dreadful circumstances. But as the three of them became more accustomed to one another, Ginny tried to create opportunities, at mealtimes or when they sat around the fire reading, painting their nails, darning their stockings, writing letters home, for Sue to enter the conversation. Had it just been the two of them in the cottage before Ginny arrived? How many other girls worked on the base? Stuck out in Section Four, she was forming only the haziest impressions of life elsewhere. But the chink in the door her questions created never widened and the dead girl never came in, and in time, the silence around her became impenetrable, as if she had never been there. The room took on the scent of Ginny's Bronnley lily-of-the-valley talcum powder, her dressing gown on the back of the door hung as if it had always been there, the tired mattress moulded itself to her body and erased Sue's.

A routine established itself. On workdays, Ginny was always first to the bathroom; as the most recent addition to the household, she had no lying-in privileges and her morning rituals were the briefest. She had never worn make-up other than the lightest smear of lipstick on special occasions, her hair, which was coarse and wilful, failed to respond to curlers, her wardrobe was as straightened as her circumstances. She had neither a father in America to send her parcels of Levi's and baseball shoes nor Alicia's ability to worship at the altar of her Singer treadle machine and conjure up miracles of transformation. Frank, though, was often up before she was; she liked to go out running, she said. The girls worked from Monday to Saturday lunchtime and on Saturday afternoons would often go out cycling, or shopping and then to the cinema in Ipswich. For Alicia and Frank this was clearly slumming it, but Ginny enjoyed the Kardomah and buying stationery in Woolworths.

On Sundays, it was expected they would go to church. In the back row of pews, where Frank and Alicia always insisted they sit in order to make a quick getaway, Ginny would survey the  worshippers in front of her. In the first pew, recognised only as a row of tweedy shoulders, the Van Heppel family who lived at Aldeford Manor and were in some way related to Alicia, with whom they would sometimes chat briefly in the churchyard after the service. Ginny was not introduced. Then a rank of Brylcreemed hair and Air Force blue collars, Adrian and his wife bookending their three daughters, scrubbed and braided, Jonathan and RichardHarryBill in their ill-fitting slope-shouldered suits (David was Jewish). It seemed to her a cosmic irony that brought them, these builders of bombs and of shelters for bombs, these listeners to the cold chatter of the Cold War, to a church dedicated to Saint Jude, patron of lost causes. Sometimes, when her mind floated free of the familiar calls and responses of morning service, she felt the density of the air around her change, as if some new element had entered it, and she fancied ironic laughter teased her ears and the sea washed through her veins, throwing her off-balance.

Even as spring advanced into summer, the church, whose walls were mapped with patches of damp, had to be heated by paraffin stoves, whose fumes, Ginny thought, probably accounted for these occasional fugue states more than any religious transportation. On a fine Sunday in August, she decided to take a walk on the castle mound after church, to clear her lungs. To think she had been living at Briar Cottage for five months and had still not explored the castle; whenever she proposed walking that way with her housemates, Frank would suggest they took the bicycles and went further afield, and she would demur. It was kind of Frank to want to show her the country.

'I'm making Yorkshire puddings,' Alicia called after her. Ginny smiled; Alicia's Yorkshire puddings were a triumph of hope over adversity but Ginny admired her perseverance.

'I'll be back before they have a chance to sink, promise.'

Frank emitted a sound somewhere between a snort and a bark, definable only by its scepticism, though whether about the puddings or Ginny's timekeeping, Ginny couldn't tell.

The close-cropped grass on the mound glittered in a mild breeze. Ginny strode up towards the castle, gulping down lungfuls of the clean, salty air. A group of good fat lambs scattered before her, scurrying back to their mothers, who lifted their heads briefly from grazing to fix her with their ancient, baleful gaze. In the lee of the castle it was suddenly so quiet she could hear the sheep tearing at the grass, and curlew song bubbling up through the clear sky. But a dense chill persisted close to the tower, seeming almost physically to shoulder her away from its arched and empty doorway. Nothing there anyway, as far as she could see, other than tamped earth, sheep droppings and a rubble of collapsed walls. Stepping out from the tower's shadow, she gazed towards the sea, raising her hand to shield her eyes from the sun. A haze was gathering to the east, a smoky violet blur on the horizon. The weather would not hold.

'Storm coming.'

Had she spoken aloud? Momentarily dazzled, she struggled to see where the words had come from before her eyes made out a man seated on a folding camp stool with an easel set up in front of him and another stool at his side holding paints and brushes. He had a brush in his left hand and a thumbhole palette in his right. She could not see what he was painting but found herself more curious about him than his work. His skin was so pale she fancied it translucent, the fine bones of cheek, nose and jaw visible beneath it. His eyes were large and deep set but she could not have told you what colour they were. It was a beautiful face, yet somehow disturbing, and it took her a little while to understand that this was because his features were unnaturally regular, as if he were himself a work of the imagination. Yet he was real enough, a man with powerful shoulders and broad, sinuous hands. The thumb holding the palette bore a blue-green paint stain.

'And here you are,' he continued.

'And here I am.'

'No,' he said, as if answering a question she had not asked. At least, she didn't think she had. 'I wasn't expecting you. At least, not in the conventional sense. When I set up, you see, I never know what I'm going to paint, what will bring everything together into a coherent image. So I wait.'

'Do you ever wait in vain?'

'Never. Waiting is its own reward, as long as you know how to do it, and I have had a lot of practice.' A gust of wind blew his hair across his face. Though it was thin on the top of his head, he wore it long, to his shoulders, as if he were a gipsy in a ballad, and it fell in very pale ropes of curl, not unlike that of the crucified Christ painted on the wall of the lady chapel in Saint Jude's. He put down his brush and tucked the stray hair behind his perfect whorled ears. 'The trick,' he continued, 'is to wait actively, openly, and opportunities come.'

Surely this was nonsense, because how could waiting be anything but passive? And yet, as she looked into his eyes, it was as if she looked through him into some perverse wonderland where sense was the opposite of what she believed it to be and the mathematical principles on which she had built her life collapsed into uncertainty. Then he blinked and the revelation was gone, its logic dissipated like that of a nightmare. 'So,' she asked, bringing herself back into the ordinariness of the summer afternoon, 'am I your opportunity? Are you going to paint me?' She was flattered to be thought a fit subject for a painting; she was not an especially pretty girl nor one for whom clothes were anything more than useful. It was difficult to imagine what this exotic man must see in her, a sturdy young woman in a sensible dress and flat sandals from Clarks.

'Perhaps not directly,' said the Artist, and her vanity shrivelled like a left-behind party balloon. 'I'm sure you have plans for your day of rest which do not include sitting for a portrait with a sou'westerly getting up. But whatever I do will contain you in some way.'

Did she want to be contained? 'Will I be able to see it when it's finished?'

A spasm of doubt crossed his face. 'Ah, well, I'm not sure when I shall pass this way again. I'm never sure. But perhaps, perhaps, if you're still here when I do.' His expression lightened again. 'And now, I believe I hear someone calling you.'

They were on the far side of the mound, with the castle between them and the lane. Did the old building set up some kind of echo? If that were the case, surely she would be able to hear a voice from the cottage as well. The Artist must have extraordinarily acute hearing. Glancing at her watch, she realised, with a pang of guilt, that the Yorkshire puddings would most likely be flat as pancakes by now.

'Well, goodbye, then,' she said, wondering if she should offer her hand. But he had turned back to his easel as if he had already forgotten her, or at least, her as she was rather than who she might become in his imagination. It was only when she was hurrying down the other side of the mound to confront Alicia's mournful wilting at the front door that she realised she had never told the Artist her name. So how had he been so certain it was her who was being called?

'The puddings have collapsed,' said Alicia with an air of resignation.

'You should have gone ahead without me. I'm sorry I'm late but…'

'To be honest, they were rather beyond redemption, despite my dutifully listening to at least half the sermon. I don't think the oven was hot enough. I think the door seal is going rotten. I'll have to speak to Drummond about it.'

'…I met a man…an Artist. He wants to paint me.'

'You? Crikey. Frank, did you hear that? Someone wants to paint Ginny's portrait.'

Frank looked up briefly from the carving or, reflected Ginny, thinking of her father's meticulous precision with his whetted blade, the ripping to shreds. Her pencilled brows arched up almost to her hairline but all she said was, 'Breast or leg?'

'Oh don't be like that, Frank.' Alicia rested her elbows on the table and balanced her chin on her hands, her meal ignored as she fixed her lilac eyes on Ginny. 'I think it's romantic. I've never been anyone's muse.' Ginny thought of Bonn, but he didn't seem the artistic type.

'Well…he was quite strange-looking.' She felt immediately the inadequacy of her words. Perhaps, if you looked like the Artist, you were condemned to live always with the inadequacy of words, and that was why he painted.

'You're blushing,' Frank accused, 'must have been strange in a good way.'

'I…I don't know.'

'Describe him. Maybe we've seen him around.'

'Maybe we already know him.' Alicia's eyes widened. She speared a carrot and held it aloft.

'I can't.'

'What do you mean?' asked Frank sharply.

'I just can't.'

'Struck dumb by Cupid's arrow,' said Alicia. 'How absolutely lovely. You must invite him round. We can hang your portrait over the fireplace.'

'Don't either of you have a boyfriend?' Ginny needed to deflect attention from the Artist before Frank and Alicia had her married off and a mother of two. Alicia gave an odd, whinnying laugh, an ugly sound that jarred with her beautiful face.

'Lord,' she said, 'No-one would marry me, not the way I cook.'

'Bonn would,' said Ginny.

'Ah, Bonn.' Noticing a hangnail, Alicia tore it off with her teeth then sucked away the blood which appeared in the quick.

'Girls shouldn't marry,' Frank asserted. 'Marriage is a conspiracy of the patriarchy.'

'The what?' asked Ginny.

'The patriarchy! You know, men. The monstrous regiment of.' Ginny, who was unfamiliar with Knox's phrase and had never thought of men other than in the individual and differentiated sense – her father, her annoying younger brother, a boy at college by whom she had felt flattered until it dawned on her he only wanted to pick her brains to improve his grades – was mystified. Frank, it seemed, was fighting a private war of her own within the larger context. She wondered what went on in the USAF building, a small corrugated hut at the northern end of the base which flew a Stars and Stripes almost big enough to cover its roof had you taken it down and stretched it across. Certainly the men who came in and out of it tended to be taller than everyone else and shout louder and have more money to spend, but she wasn't sure that justified describing them as monstrous. Or a regiment. Ginny had never been into their hut but she thought there was only around half a dozen of them.

Frank was watching her, a challenging spark in her eye, one eyebrow gallantly raised. She expected a response. Alicia, still sucking her finger, was no help.

'Right,' Ginny said, not wanting to betray ignorance, 'I see.'

'But you don't, that's obvious. I suppose you're like Alicia, an optimist. You believe men are softened and tamed by marriage, but they're not. Instead, they drag you down to their level,' she paused, staring at her plate, picking absently at a loose thread in the tablecloth, and her voice dropped as if in tune with her words, 'into the dark.'

'It's because her parents are divorced,' said Alicia, rather spitefully, Ginny thought. Perhaps Bonn was better off without her.

The remainder of lunch passed in an atmosphere as heavy and flat as the Yorkshire puddings. Afterwards, Frank said she was going out to make a phone call, leaving Alicia and Ginny to do the washing up without her.

'Just like a man herself, one might say,' Alicia muttered, scrubbing at a plate as if to remove its pattern.

'Why are you here?' asked Ginny. 'I mean, you and Frank, you don't need the money, do you? And you're not...I mean, you could work anywhere if you wanted to. London. A nice flat with clean tea towels,' she added in an attempt to lighten the atmosphere.

'It was Frank's idea. She found out they were looking for people. I just sort of...tagged along.'

'Have you known Frank for a long time?'

'We were at school together.'

Ginny experienced an inner quailing before the fortifications erected by that phrase, the feeling it conjured of being an irredeemable outsider. 'Ah,' she said, though Alicia didn't seem to hear her. She stood with her rubber-gloved hands plunged into the dishwater and gazed dreamily out of the steamed-up kitchen window which gave on to the wall surrounding the back yard of the pub.

'She came late, when she was fifteen, and she was so exotic. And forceful! She had opinions, you know? I didn't have many friends...'

'I find that hard to believe,' Ginny blurted out, 'you're so...'

'Beautiful, I know.' She sighed and her shoulders dropped as though beauty were an intolerable burden. 'I hate it, Ginny. People treat you oddly, as if you're breakable, or came from outer space, or have a contagious illness. It's an absolute curse. I started biting my nails to make me more normal, you know and now, well, it's become a habit.' She handed Ginny a plate for drying. 'I don't feel I can do anything, I just am.'

'You're a wonder with that sewing machine.'

Alicia brightened a little. 'Ah yes, I love sewing. It's transformative, you see. I can't turn myself into anything else but I can take a length of fabric or an old frock and make it new. That machine is vintage, you know, fifty years old or so. I bought it from a funny little man in Felixstowe when I came down here.'

'I assumed you'd brought it with you, some sort of heirloom. I realised it was old; my grandmother had one similar.'

'God no! Using a sewing machine was awfully frowned upon at home. Fine to do a bit of needlepoint of an evening but not machine sewing. A pronounced whiff of factory work, d'you see?' Ginny did; her grandmother had taken in piecework during the Depression and didn't doubt her children would have starved to death without it.

'Well,' said Ginny, 'I think it's a terrific skill. Useful and, if I'm allowed to say so, beautiful.'

'Ah, William Morris.'

'Who?'

Alicia gave her a quizzical look and thrust another plate at her. 'Never mind,' she said.

It was long after they had finished clearing away when Frank returned. Ginny had gone up to her room to write a letter home. Her eye caught by movement outside her window, she watched Frank walking up the lane from the direction of the sea, which struck her as odd if Frank had been out to use the phonebox in the square. Perhaps she had gone for a walk and was returning just in the nick of time. The light behind the tower was an oppressive purple, the air dense with the threat of the coming storm.

# 5

They woke on Monday to rain flung against the windows with a clatter like thrown pebbles. The wind had reached down the chimney and scattered cold ashes all over the hearth rug. It had blown out the pilot light on the cooker and everywhere, to Ginny, seemed imbued with the rotten egg reek of Calor gas. Frank insisted it was just damp, with such authority that Ginny imagined the gas creeping back into the cylinder outside the kitchen door, shamed by daring to contradict her.

'Will the boats cross in this?' she asked, suddenly anxious. After her disconcerting encounter with the Artist and her sad conversation with Alicia the previous evening, she felt out of sorts and longed for her calculations and the benign anarchy of Section Four.

'Oh God, yes,' answered Frank. 'It would have to be Noah's flood to stop work on the Island. After all, the Russians can build bombs in Siberia.'

'Siberia has permafrost.' Ginny thought of the Island, so low to the water it was little more than a sandbar, a wrinkle the sea might smooth out in moments. Frank threw her an unreadable glance.

They couldn't get the pilot light relit so they left all the downstairs windows open; before they had even quit the house, water had begun to soak into the carpet below the sitting room window. Noticing the spreading stains as she buttoned her gabardine, Ginny was briefly shaken by the notion that it emanated from the castle, looming beyond the window behind a billowing grey curtain of rain. As if the building were bleeding. The words seemed not to be hers but to have arrived among her thoughts from somewhere outside herself.

The channel was choppy and the wind, once they were clear of land, knifed through her damp clothes. Though the small boat bucked and tossed alarmingly, Ginny's body felt rigid with cold, her hands in an arthritic curl, her jaw set. But she was a good sailor, she had discovered, and found a bleak magnificence in the iron sea punching up into the bellying cloud and the mysterious blur of the Island, no more than a thickening of the turbulent air, always receding, it seemed, at the same pace their small craft crept forward. Sea birds tossed about like windblown scraps of paper. Strands of Frank's bright hair escaped from beneath her rain hat, red hot wires woven through the vista of greys. A head bobbed darkly in the tail of her eye before plunging back beneath the waves, a seal, sleek, wild spirit of the storm.

'This is madness,' muttered David, huddled next to her, his glasses encrusted with salt. Behind them, somebody retched and he dropped his head into his hands with a groan. 'That's all we need.'

'Buck up, David,' Ginny urged him, 'we're almost

there.' And looking ahead, to check the veracity of her statement, again, among the sea's peaks and troughs, she saw the dark head, now there, now gone.

The strip of sand under the landing stage was littered with flotsam, clumps of weed like knots of tousled hair, bits of broken wood, rope, nets and glitterings of glass shards, a starfish, its flesh-pink limbs writhing in bewilderment. A pebble caught her eye, a flint whose facets reflected the rain's shine. She picked it up and found it had a hole worn through it.

'A hagstone,' said Phin, coming up beside her. 'They say if you look through it you can see the future.' Remembering the similar stone Phin kept on his desk to restrain the cascade of his working papers, she wondered what future it showed him. She held hers up to one eye and trained it on the starfish, whose limbs were now spread lifeless on the sand. She thrust it into her coat pocket.

As they crossed the spine of the Island, the exotic silhouettes of the pagodas emerged into view. The rain had darkened the concrete to the colour of wet earth; you could imagine they were as old as the castle yet they had only been in existence a matter of weeks. Ginny was proud of the pagodas; however whimsical they appeared with their convex roofs and pillared supports clustered like groves of small trees (Phin's follies they were dubbed by the rest of the base), they were the end result of months of collaborative calculation and modelling to find the structure most likely to withstand the blast impact of a Russian ICBM. They were emblematic of this team of oddballs and misfits among whom she had found her place. She paused and held up the hagstone to them, and it seemed to bring them into sharper focus.

'We'll not be out there today,' said Phin. 'A day for slide rules and tea and biscuits, I think.'

What was that? A glimpse, a flash of wind-whipped fiery brightness. Frank's hair, it looked like, but what would Frank be doing out by the pagodas? And how could she have got there so soon after the boats had landed?

'Ginny? Everything alright?' asked Phin.

'Yes, yes, fine. Sorry. They're rather absorbing these things, aren't they?'

'Sometimes,' said Phin, 'I find the restricted view a relief.'

Ginny smiled at him. 'Slide rules and tea and biscuits,' she repeated; perhaps not a prospect to everyone's taste but certainly to theirs. She paused to re-align one of the white marker stones, even though the path itself had been almost entirely washed away by the wind and rain.

'I like your optimism.' Phin turned his face to the open sea, squinting his eyes to protect them from the needling rain. 'Do you ever think it strange that we came up with precisely that roof shape? Like something you might see in a Japanese tea garden?'

'It's the maths, Phin, you know that.'

'Just makes you wonder, you know, if there's more to the maths than meets the eye.'

'The maths makes the bombs, the maths makes the shelters. That's all.'

'Ah, there's no poetry in your soul, Ginny Matlock.'

'Probably just as well where nuclear weapons are concerned.'

'You don't sometimes wonder if we should be reading Chekhov and Tolstoy? Trying to understand the Russian soul?' Ginny gave an emphatic shake of her head and hoped Phin wasn't losing his grip.

'Just joking,' he said, landing a light punch on her arm as if she were one of the boys. They walked on, past the lake and down the shallow slope towards Section Four. The sea moaned and spasmed like a great, sick beast.

Though Ginny managed to stay focused on her work, the storm did not quite loosen its grip on her consciousness. It acted as a chaotic counterpoint to the elegant symmetry of the equations she was working on, it snarled and roiled behind the tidy march of figures across the squared grid of her pad. And the flash of Frank's hair against rain-darkened concrete kept coming back to her. Eventually, telling her alarmed and mystified colleagues she needed to clear her head, she went outside. As she was putting on her outdoor clothes, just beside her an egg carton clapped to the floor, shaken loose by the wind rattling the flimsy corrugated walls.

'You'll catch your death from something,' warned Jonathan.

'Ach, I'm from Manchester. It's like this all the time up there.'

'Statistically,' retorted Jonathan drily, 'I doubt that's true.'

'And we don't deal in unfounded impressions?' They laughed, but she found herself reflecting, as she wrapped her scarf around her neck, that she seemed to have fallen prey to all kinds of unfounded impressions and that there were a great many things on the Island from which one might die.

Of course there was nothing to be seen outside, other than the display the weather was putting on. Rain smudged the outlines of clouds as if some celestial hand had swept across a page of wet black ink. An opaque sea broke against the shore and scattered its fragments into the air. A colossal roaring and snarling and screaming suffocated the smaller sounds of rigging slapping against masts and flagpoles, the cries of seabirds, the rushing of water through drifts of pebbles as the elements set about remodelling the Island. If Ginny turned her back to the wind, she could lean against it as if it had the solidity of a chair back while everything around her was in flux. Once the novelty of this retreated in the face of water soaking through her scarf and dripping down the back of her neck, she went back inside. Papers flew and people swore as the wind barged in beside her.

There was no tea because their power went out, and by the time they were battling their way to the canteen for lunch, it was out across the base. Trays of sandwiches had been laid out in the guttering light of candles and storm lanterns. Drummond, with a bedraggled Alicia at his side, stood in front of the serving hatch waiting to address them all.

'I'm very sorry, everyone, but the met wallahs have informed me this is set in for the next twelve hours or so. I'm therefore cancelling tonight's boats and arrangements will be made to put you all up on the base. Our phone lines are down but the radio is working and Alicia here will be happy to get messages to your families on shore.'

Alicia stepped forward, brandishing a notebook and a tiny golden pencil, the sort that came with novelty address books. Ginny found it improbable that Alicia should possess anything so tasteless and immediately even more improbable that she should be thinking that way. Clearly, living with Frank and Alicia was having more influence on her than she was aware of. She helped herself to sandwiches and squash, and watched as Alicia moved around the tables taking details of everyone who needed to be contacted. Mutterings of discontent and some mildly hysterical laughter competed with the rattling of the windows in their frames and the canteen staff banging about behind the serving hatch. Frank emerged from somewhere in the restless shadows and sat down at Ginny's table, telling David and Jonathan to shove along and make room.

'Golly,' she said, putting on an accent closer to Noël Coward's than her own, 'it'll be just like Mallory Towers.'

Ginny resented her mocking tone; she had enjoyed the Mallory Towers books, but as Frank had actually attended a boarding school Ginny supposed she was entitled to her irreverence.

'Did I see you out by the pagodas earlier?' she asked. Frank certainly looked windblown, but then, they all did, so her tangled curls and rain-marked shoulders were no indication of anything. Her sudden blush, though, gave the lie to her words.

'I don't think so, no. I've been at my desk all morning. My guys are whirling around like rudderless boats because they've lost their connection to the Pentagon.' She broke into a few bars of Motherless Child but tailed off into weak laughter when her singing elicited no response from Ginny.

'I was sure I did. Your hair...there's no-one else with hair that colour on the base.'

'No, Gin.' She fixed Ginny with her green gaze, more ice today than birch leaves. 'You didn't.' She picked up a ham sandwich as if that were the end of the conversation, took a bite, and flung it back on to the plate. 'My God, that's disgusting!'

She was rattled and Ginny, who disliked being lied to, felt like a dog with a rabbit to worry. 'Tell me about Sue,' she said. Now the colour drained completely from Frank's face.

'She...she left. Got another job. It didn't seem important. You never asked if we'd shared with anyone before. I wonder why you're asking now?'

'Because I heard different. I heard she'd drowned. I wonder why you wouldn't mention that, unless it wasn't an accident?'

'Oh don't be ridiculous. Section Four must be getting to you. People say it does.' She paused, raised that single questioning eyebrow. 'Makes one wonder just what you get

43

up to in there?' Ginny had a sudden, chilling sensation of being alone with Frank, as if only she and Frank and the rising storm remained on the Island, everyone else plucked up and whirled away by the wind and waves. Later, she wondered what she might have said if Alicia had not plumped herself down beside Frank, her ridiculous pencil in the corner of her mouth and a plate of pink wafer biscuits in her hand.

'Darlings. Isn't this fun?'

# 6

The men were billeted in the canteen and the ten civilian women who worked on the base in the small sick bay. Ginny quickly gained the impression this routine was not unfamiliar to them. Someone had smuggled a packet of digestive biscuits and a tin of jam out of the canteen. Frank moved without hesitation to one of the bedside cabinets and brought out of it a bottle of Famous Grouse and a pack of cards.

'Strip poker,' she announced. Ginny quailed.

'I think I'll...' she began but nobody was listening. They were already busy negotiating the rules at the tops of their voices. One shoe at a time or the pair? Just down to underwear or all the way?

'All the way!' shouted Frank, and while hesitancy clouded some faces, most whooped and laughed and started organising themselves into a playing circle.

In the Mallory Towers books the plain, clever girl

always triumphed but not here. It was Frank's fault. Ginny quickly calculated that she wasn't dealing straight, but because she failed to spot her sleight of hand, she couldn't call her out. The candles had scarcely burned down at all by the time everyone except Frank was in an advanced stage of undress, transformed by the guttering light into a tableau of flesh and silk lingerie which put Ginny in mind of something she might have seen on a school trip to the Whitworth Art Gallery. She herself sat with her knees drawn up to her chest to hide the folds of her belly, mortified by her sensible Saint Michael bra and pants, increasingly uncomfortable in the company of Frank, who occasionally glanced her way with an oddly expectant, inquisitive expression.

'I should really buy more sensible underwear,' sighed one long-limbed thoroughbred of a girl whom Ginny didn't know but thought she might have seen in the Quartermaster's store when she went once to collect pencils. 'The hard water here wreaks havoc with silk.'

Thankfully, the game petered out quite quickly because no-one wanted to be the first to strip naked and everyone was getting cold. The girls lounged around, sweaters and cardigans thrown over their slips, drinking whisky, eating digestives spread with tinned jam, which glowed a disturbing electric pink in the candlelight, talking about films and fashion, pop stars and boyfriends. Having nothing to contribute to the conversation and sensing the onset of a headache, Ginny gathered up her clothes and went next door into the nurse's office to change.

Only one candle burned in there, but it was a fat church candle set in a saucer and gave off a good light. By it she could appreciate the room's orderliness and felt the pressure begin to lift from her temples. She realised her jaw was clenched and made a deliberate effort to relax it, hoping to ward off the headache. Yet as she surveyed the clear desk, the instruments neatly lined up in the autoclave, and let the silence seep into her, there remained a disturbance at the corner of her vision, a sort of fraying, a sense of something not quite seen, not quite understood. She dressed. The silence sank down through her, letting in the pebble-scatter of rain against the window, the snarl of the wind chewing at the corners of the building. She peered out at the square of night, leaned against the pane…

…and saw a face peering in. Her own, it must be, in the dark mirror. And yet… This was a man's face, with broad, strong bones and large eyes beneath unusually regular brows, and long, pale hair curling over his shoulders, whipping across his face in the wind. It wasn't her reflection she saw in the window, but only, doubled and reduced, in the eyes of the Artist. What could he be doing out there in such weather? How had he even managed to make the crossing? Had he been here all along? Perhaps he lived here, somewhere below the radar of the base, in one of the unexplained buildings left over from the war, no longer in use and skulking beneath thick pelts of ivy and Russian vine. But if that were the case, why was he outside this window now? Well, her questions would have to wait. The main thing now was to get him indoors, out of the storm. There was an external door in the nurse's office, but when she tried it, she found it was locked. He would have to climb in through the window. She set about its catch with stiff fingers, then suddenly the wind snatched it away from her and flung it wide. She leaned out. No sign of the Artist. Had the window caught him and knocked him over as it swung open? Was he now lying unconscious out there? She couldn't just leave him, not in such a storm.

Hauling herself on to the sill, she balanced a moment, her left arm raised against the furious banging of the window, the air sucked from her lungs by the wind, the rain lashing at her then finding its way around her, into the room. The smash of glass from somewhere behind her. She glanced over her shoulder on a reflex and saw a flask which had been standing beside the autoclave had crashed to the floor. She lifted one leg over the sill.

'Ginny.' For a second she failed to recognise the voice as Frank's. The tone was flat, robotic almost, quite lacking her housemate's usual hectic animation. She looked around. What she saw frightened her.

'I was just…I thought I saw that Artist out there but now I don't know…'

'Well go on then,' said Frank. 'Go out and take a look.' Frank's eyes glittered, as if all her mercurial personality was suddenly focused there, leaving this dulled voice, the unnatural stillness of her, standing so close to Ginny she could smell her breath, a combination of whisky and the boiled sweet stink of the jam. The light seemed even to have gone out of her hair, leaving nothing but the smoulder of a dying fire. 'Go. No-one wants you here. If the sea's calling, listen to it.' She gave a bitter laugh. 'Do the rational thing.'

Ginny was feeling the cold now. She could imagine the blood in her veins mixed with crushed ice, like the Crème de Menthe frappés her mother drank once a year, after Christmas lunch. Was this what had happened to Sue? Was this why no-one talked about her? Was Sue like her? A misfit. She felt homesick. Washing day at the villa in Didsbury, the sudsy fug in the scullery, the familiar squeak of the mangle, whose handle her father was forever going to oil. Her mother singing music hall numbers to the twintub and conducting herself with the laundry tongs. The scent of bed linen fresh off the line, cheap jam, whisky…falling…no, not falling but being pushed, squeezed between Frank's weight and the weight of the wind until she could no longer breathe…a drowning girl…Sue…Was this what had happened to Sue? Had Frank…?

'Hey, I heard glass breaking. Are you having a party in here without me?' Alicia. Thank God. Frank stepped away from the window. Ginny swung her leg back inside. Wherever they had been, they were back in the world of dormitory confidences and late-night card games now. Ginny leaned out to grasp the madly swinging window, pulled it in and fastened it, leaving the wind to shoulder at it uselessly. Though her gaze was repeatedly drawn to check, she could see nothing now but the oblong of blackness.

'The window blew open.' It was a lame explanation, but Alicia seemed willing to believe it.

'We could do with a dustpan,' she said, taking a ledger from the desk and using it to push the broken glass into a pile beside the wastepaper basket.

'Yes,' said Frank, and began hunting through cupboards. Ginny watched them, wondering if she was mad or if they were. The window rattled in its frame. Was the Artist really out there, a creature of wind and rain and the ever restless sea? Had Frank killed Sue? Why? The frayed corner of her vision. The hoop tightening again at her temples.

'Forget that, Frank. Get Ginny some whisky. She doesn't look at all well.'

Frank did as she was told. The whisky tasted of the plastic tooth mug in which it was served and Ginny felt it moving through her like a stream between rocks. The girls returned to the ward; as Frank pushed open the door she began to laugh, and after a few seconds, Alicia joined her, just as if the three of them were in the middle of an amusing conversation. In the ward the others were chatting about the Van Heppel Christmas Ball; as soon as the August bank holiday ended, it seemed, they must turn their attention to ball gowns. Ginny lay on her bed and fell into a shallow, restless sleep, in which the talk around her insinuated itself into her dreams. Dreams in which Wing Commander Drummond ordered her, with Frank's voice, into a boat, which became a train, taking her home. She cried out in protest, let me stay, I like work better than Christmas, but her words were drowned out by the train, which roared like the furious sea. Dreams in which she could smell boiled sprouts and lavender bags and wondered why her wardrobe was full of her old school skirts and blouses and the blind ex-servicemen who waltzed down the street to the strains of the Blue Danube, selling the lavender bags door to door. Dreams in which bombs smacked into the beach outside Section Four, sending up plumes of sand that blanketed the atmosphere and scarfed up the sun and there were no more lavender bags.

When morning came, and with it an exhausted calm, she felt as if she had not slept at all. She was grateful when Wing Commander Drummond announced that, as it was Friday, they would work a short day. Civilian personnel would be taken off the Island at midday, leaving the military to clear up after the storm. The headache which had begun the previous evening worsened, and her rows of calculations jumped in front of her eyes like fleas in a circus. She dragged through the morning, sluggish and dull, and was scarcely aware of crossing to the landing stage to catch the boat, until she realised that where habit wanted her feet to take her, there was no longer any path. Stepping into a drift of sand, she stumbled, which brought her to her senses. The path, with its raked shingle and whitewashed stone markers, had been completely erased by the storm. Already, small wading birds were picking through the sand for whatever the sea might have tossed up that they could eat; they took no notice of Ginny as she reversed her steps and began to follow the others who had made a new route which skirted the drift. She kept her distance. She avoided getting into the same boat as Frank.

As soon as the girls reached the cottage, Ginny went

to bed. The stairs seemed insurmountable yet she forced her legs to carry her up them, driven by a need to escape her housemates, to find some peace in which to wonder what had actually happened during the night of the storm. She dropped her clothes where she stood, but they were damp and she knew she couldn't settle unless she spread them out to air. Stooping to gather them up, her back stiff and her brain swilling in her skull, her eye was caught by something small and bright wedged between one rear leg of the desk and the dusty skirting board. She picked it up. It was a fine gold chain bearing a single pearl. A chill shuddered along her spine as she realised it must have belonged to Sue. A breeze seemed to agitate the curtain between the living and the dead and afford her a glimpse of the other side.

There was a knock on the door and the curtain settled again. Thrusting the pendant into her dressing gown pocket she called,

'Come in.'

'I brought you this.' Frank, holding out a hot water bottle. A peace offering? Or was it intended to scald her? The girls edged towards one another until Ginny could reach out at arm's length and grab the hot water bottle. 'Look,' Frank continued, 'about yesterday…be warned.'

Ginny clutched the hot water bottle to her chest like a shield. 'What do you mean?'

'I can't say more. I've already said more than I should. Just sometimes…bad things must be done for the sake of the greater good.'

The cold, damp air of the room seeped into Ginny's bones. The futile hiss of the Aladdin filled the silence between the girls.

'And pushing me out of a window was for the greater good, was it? Or perhaps you didn't even see it as a bad thing?' With her free hand she clutched at the necklace in her pocket; she imagined the answer to the riddle of Sue coiled inside the pearl like the answer to a riddle in a Christmas cracker. Words and gunpowder.

'I didn't push you,' said Frank, levelling her green gaze at Ginny. 'Whatever happened was in your own mind. You were half way out of that window when I came in.'

'There was someone outside! I was trying to help him!'

'No.' Frank shook her head. 'There was no-one.' Again, that flat, emphatic tone, the deep, steady gaze. It was almost as if Frank were trying to hypnotise her, to erase her memory of the previous night and replace it with something else. Her last remark hung in the air as Ginny closed the door behind her. She thought Frank was probably on drugs. Her mother, divorced from her father, was part of what Alicia called 'that Chelsea Arts set' in London. Ginny was going to ask for new digs. Tomorrow, she would ask Bonn; he handled that kind of thing for the Wing Commander. Tomorrow, once she had had a decent night's sleep, everything would seem more straightforward.

Yet the conversation haunted her. She chased its meaning around and around in her head but could not catch it. What warning was Frank trying to give her? Could she be a Communist? Ginny thought again of the Chelsea Arts set. Or maybe she was with the American secret services. That jeep, which seemed to be at her disposal whenever she wanted it. The parcels from her father. But they were our allies, surely. Thoughts spinning, Ginny broke out in an anxious sweat, but the core of her, where the hot water bottle could not reach, was freezing cold. Her head was pounding, all her limbs ached and she could think no further than putting one foot in front of the other until she was close enough to the bed to fall on to it. At some point she was dimly aware of having crawled under the bed covers. The Artist peered at her through the hole in the hagstone, though he would neither confirm nor deny having been outside the sick bay on the night of the storm. You're just ashamed you did nothing to defend me from Frank, she accused him. You are indefensible, I'm afraid, he said, in Frank's voice. You need a doctor.

Sue was there, blue-veined and water-veiled, her hair drifting around her head like weed in a current, threaded with tiny, pearlescent fishes. There was a hectic glitter in her eyes as she leaned over Ginny and pressed the stethoscope to her chest, but when Ginny looked again, the little fishes darted in her empty sockets. Rest, said Sue, and you'll be fit as a fiddle in no time. Alicia swam to the surface of her consciousness, saying something about the Van Heppel ball, then dissolved into the myriad facets of a kaleidoscope, waltzing together, swirling apart. Her bedroom floor became music, her bed supported by a net of notes woven by violin players wielding their bows as shuttles. She had to pull herself together, to be ready for when the music stopped.

She knew, when she woke, that she had been dreaming for a long time. The return of consciousness felt like a return from somewhere far away and long ago.

# 7

The cottage was empty when she came downstairs, on legs as shaky as a newborn foal's, to go to the bathroom. At first, she thought Frank and Alicia had gone out cycling or taken the jeep into Ipswich, but, when she glanced at the calendar on the back of the kitchen door, she discovered it was Tuesday and September had begun.

When she had finished in the bathroom, she slowly made herself a cup of tea and stood looking out of the sitting room window towards the castle as she drank it and waited for its restorative properties to work on her. The day was oppressive and still; even the gulls seemed subdued, drooped along the castle's crenellated roof as if the air were too heavy for them. The tower itself loomed darkly, its walls patched with salt stains and rusty lichen. In its shadow, Ginny felt like a wraith, as if even the slightest draft under the front door might blow her to dust. She added several spoons of sugar to her tea, ate some toast and marmalade, and felt the energy tingle back into her limbs. Her blood flowed sluggish and thick; she needed fresh air. She decided on a short walk over the castle mound.

A fine drizzle blurred the view but the outdoors invigorated her. As she climbed the mound, she settled into her stride, and wondered if she might have the strength to walk down to the harbour to meet the boats. Then she stopped dead in her tracks.

There was the Artist, sitting at his easel, apparently oblivious to the weather, though he was wearing a long, dark coat with the collar turned up and his curls snaked out from beneath a close-fitting woollen cap. Ginny blinked, half expecting him to be gone when she opened her eyes again, but he remained. She thought of turning tail and running back to the cottage, but her feet kept walking towards him, as though his mind was controlling her rather than her own. Her ears were filled with the faint hiss of the rain, like radio interference, and her surroundings lost their familiarity, flowed away from her until only she and the Artist and the patch of ground that held them remained. She tried to cling on; whatever she thought she had seen outside the sickbay window on the night of the storm, it must have been an hallucination brought on by her illness. Neither Frank nor Alicia had seen him; that was the only rational explanation. The Artist was here, now, but he had not been on the Island that night. Even so, she didn't believe herself.

'The lunar girl, orbiting this little hill like a heavenly body,' said the Artist, and the rain's hiss abruptly ceased. He turned to look at her. There was a phosphorescent smoulder in his eyes. He smiled, flicked his tongue quickly over his lips as if they were dry.

'I'm not sure I like your tone.'

He sagged a little with disappointment. 'I expected you to take words at their face value, a girl like you, accustomed to being analytical. I meant simply that the Moon is in her last quarter, as she was the last time we met.'

Now he had explained himself she wondered if she might indeed have taken on some lunar quality, some translucence, a tendency to disappear. 'But surely we met only days ago, during the storm. Or at least, I saw you, on the Island. Perhaps you didn't see me.'

'I have never been on the Island as such.'

'Well, I suppose no-one without authorisation can really go there so…'

'Authorisation, yes, that's the thing. Never wise to find yourself in a place without authorisation.' His words had a bite to them, as if he meant more than he was saying.

Had she revealed too much? One set of words she was obliged to take at face value was the Official Secrets Act. He smiled at her, not, she thought, entirely kindly.

'It's alright,' he said, 'I know you work as a computer there.'

'How…?' A chill crept along her spine. Was he a Russian spy? He could be a Russian, with those looks, though to her knowledge, Ginny had never seen a Russian. That was why Frank had pretended not to see him; they were in cahoots. And Alicia? No, he had made himself scarce by the time she came in. He laughed. She had not heard him laugh before and the sound was alarming, a tuneless honk, like the conversation of beached seals.

'I admire you, envy you perhaps. Mathematics is a pure vocation. It frees one from the irrational.'

She nodded, smiled, decided it was safer, here alone with him, to play the ingénue, and report him to Drummond as soon as she returned to work.

'So,' she said brightly, 'did you paint me? I would like to see what use you made of our meeting.'

'Perhaps I made no use of it at all.'

'You seemed quite certain you would.'

'Inspiration is often transitory. Elusive. What seems compelling one moment can turn out to be meaningless as soon as the light changes. However, as it happens, you did find your way on to my page.'

'Can I see?'

'I have a sketch here somewhere, I think.' He made a play of riffling through his sketchbook. When he found what he was looking for, he set it on his easel with a small flourish. Ginny stepped eagerly forward, a pleasurable flush flowing up from her chest. As her eyes took in the picture, however, anticipation shrivelled and soured.

He had made a head and shoulders drawing with charcoal on a blue-washed page, but the face was not Ginny's. It was the face of her fever-dreams, the face she knew in these dreams to be Sue's, a play of fine bones and delicate angles, haloed by floating hair. At the throat, at the centre of the shaded dip between the collarbones, hung a single pearl on a thin chain. The same pendant which, she now remembered, was still in her dressing gown pocket.

'This isn't me.' She thrust her hands into her coat pockets, fists clenched to stop them shaking. 'This isn't me.'

'Not a likeness, perhaps, but you inspired it nevertheless. Just as you wished.'

'Who are you?' she demanded. 'Who are you?'

The Artist spread his large hands, and a trick of perspective made it look as if he were about to embrace the castle. 'A neighbour.'

'No you're not. If you lived in the village I'd have seen you in the grocer's, or The Merman. You just…pop up here with your paints and things whenever I decide to go for a walk, it seems.'

'Just your impression. You see a pattern where there is

only coincidence. I am quite often in The Merman, though I notice you don't go there much.'

'No,' Ginny admitted. Her liking for the pub had not increased, and as Frank and Alicia seldom went there either, she had mostly stayed away.

'And what did you see when you called me the lunar girl? Surely you don't believe the phases of the Moon are random.'

'Nor do I believe they govern your appearances, as if you were a tide, rolling in and out on this little hill. It was merely a pleasantry.' Not, then, to be taken at face value.

Her gaze was drawn back to the portrait and she felt suddenly deathly cold. 'I fear you,' she said, 'with your glib remarks and that...that...it's not me, I don't possess a necklace like that.'

'I felt sure you did.' A light remark, yet it settled like lead in her heart.

'I have to go. I've not been well. I need to get out of the rain.' I need, she thought, the blood beating in her ears as she ran back over the mound, to get out of your net before it draws tight around me. And wondered where such a thought could have come from because the words did not seem at all like hers.

Once inside the cottage, without even removing her outdoor clothes, she crossed to the lugubrious sideboard and started opening cupboards and drawers. She felt compelled to know what Sue had looked like and wondered if there might be a photograph of her somewhere. There was no reason why there should be, Sue's parents having presumably collected her belongings, but the necklace had been overlooked so it seemed a slender possibility. She found what she knew she would find: table linen, some old bills, a toolbox which was empty except for a hammer, a bottle of gin and a cocktail shaker belonging to Frank.

There was a cutlery drawer in the dining table, and she riffled through that, emptying out the cutlery in case anything might have been concealed beneath it; she found only fluffballs and a desiccated wasp. It was the same everywhere she looked, except where the pristine Dansette gleamed under the stairs atop its crate of records, nothing but the familiar flotsam washed up by the tides of those who had flowed through Briar Cottage.

Pausing to remove her coat and boots, she wondered if she could go through Frank and Alicia's rooms, which seemed a significantly more transgressive step than excavating the shared parts of the house. She looked at her watch: two hours at least until the boats from the Island came back ashore on the mainland. Something hardened in her.

She reached Frank's door first. Her hand wavered briefly over the handle before she collected herself and pushed the door open. The drizzle had gathered, now, into rain, and she could hear it drumming on the empty beer kegs stacked in the pub yard, which was overlooked by the two back bedrooms. The room was cold and a stale, but expensive, fragrance lay heavy on the air. Clothes were heaped on the bed and one of Frank's bright red lipsticks stood on her dresser with its lid off. Tucked into the corner of the mirror was a photo of a family group on a lawn, a substantial white weatherboarded house behind them and a golden retriever laid out like a rug at their feet. Despite the plaits and the braces on her teeth, she recognised a young Frank and guessed the three red-haired boys lined up next to her in order of height must be her brothers. Happier times, she thought, or perhaps the woman in the photo, wholesomely tanned, wearing Capri pants and a crisp white shirt, was a step-mother; she looked a long way removed from Ginny's idea of the Chelsea Arts set. Somehow, the photo made Ginny feel squeamish about what she was about to do, as if all those eyes were watching her. She told herself not to be ridiculous and pulled open the top dresser drawer.

Most of the drawers contained tangles of lingerie and heaps of cosmetics, the sheer volume of which made Ginny angry for some reason she could not discern, which in turn made her angrier. She slammed each drawer shut and was about to give the last one the same treatment when she noticed the corner of another photograph peeping out from among balled socks and stockings. Blushing fiercely, she slid it out of the drawer.

It was a head and shoulders shot of two girls. The one Ginny did not recognise was looking straight to camera out of cornflower blue eyes wide set above cheekbones that swept out like swallows' wings. Slavic, they would have said in her mother's romances. Her fair hair was cut short as a boy's except for the fringe, which fell lopsidedly over one eye. She was not smiling, and her full bottom lip suggested sulkiness, though there was also something defiant in the way she was staring down the camera lens over the shoulder of her companion, whom Ginny recognised immediately from her flaming hair even though her back was turned. Frank. Both girls appeared to be naked, except for the pearl pendant worn by the unidentified blonde.

Ginny felt heat rising from her chest to her face. She ran a hand around the neck of her sweater in a futile attempt to ease it. What did this mean? Perhaps it was just some kind of artistic portrait. Frank was into modern art; she was always going on about the Hepworth at Snape. But her mind went back to the family snap in the mirror, to the bright white weatherboarding, the blue sky and green grass, the open smiles and the short, sharp shadows of midday, and something shifted in her, and she knew this was different. She carried the photo to the window and leaned her cheek against the cold glass. A shimmering halo surrounded her vision, as if her illness were returning. She closed her eyes, listened to the creaks and rattles of the old building which she normally found comforting but today increasingly convinced her there was someone else in the house. Had the others come back early for some reason? Was more bad weather forecast?

Moving as quietly as she could, she crept back to the dresser to return the photo to the drawer. As she did so, she noticed something scrawled on the back of it: the initials 'S' and 'F', a date she could not decipher and a phone number. She picked up the lipstick and copied the number on to the back of her hand. Then, fumbling in her haste to conceal the photo again under the balled socks and stockings, she dislodged a pair of socks that rolled out on to the floor. As she bent to pick it up, the bedroom door shifted on its hinges. She froze, the blood thundering in her ears. A jumble of words unrolled in her head as she tried to formulate excuses. The door sighed shut, as though exasperated by her ineptitude. She straightened up, expecting to see Frank standing there, but there was no-one, just a leavening of ozone, blown in, she supposed while the door was ajar. A stray hair danced in the draft before gliding to the floor, a hot wire gleam in the window's light. She put Frank's socks back in the drawer and, with a last look around the room to make sure she had left nothing out of place, she went downstairs and out to the telephone box in front of the greengrocers; even if there had been a phone in the cottage, something told her she wouldn't have used it.

The numbers had smudged a bit as she delved in her purse for coins but remained legible. The phone rang for some time, and she had just about resigned herself to the frustrating fact that no-one was in when a woman's voice, somewhat hesitant and questioning, said,

'Hello?'

'Mrs. Reynolds?'

A silence, just long enough to become uncomfortable, during which Ginny fancied she could hear nasal, stertorious breathing, though perhaps it was just interference on the line. She thought of hanging up, stared at a pyramid of cabbages outside the greengrocers, fading gradually as her breath misted up the panes of the phone box.

'There's no-one of that name here,' said the voice, eventually.

'I'm not speaking to Sue Reynolds' mother?'

'Who is this?'

'My name is Ginny Matlock. I've taken over...that is, I share Briar Cottage now, with Frank and Alicia.'

A gasp, and the phone went dead. Ginny removed the receiver from her ear and stared at it as if it might offer some explanation of what had just happened. In the circumstances, she would have understood if Mrs. Reynolds had been reluctant to talk about her daughter, but to deny she was Mrs. Reynolds at all? Had Ginny misread the number? But if she had dialled a wrong number, surely the woman would simply have said so. It happened all the time; that was what people did.

Outside the phone box the greengrocer was dismantling the pyramid of cabbages and winding up his awning. The light was fading early, the clouds seeming to close in around her. Frank and Alicia would be back from the Island any time now. Ginny slipped into the grocer's just as he was about to lock up and purchased half a dozen eggs. Hurrying back to the cottage, she took off her outdoor clothes, wrapped herself in a flowered apron and set about mixing a sponge. She wasn't a good cook, but she liked to bake; the need for precision appealed to her, calmed her. Besides, if her housemates came in to find her surrounded by cake ingredients, nothing would seem out of the ordinary; she would have covered the tracks leading from the Artist to the photo to her disconcerting non-conversation with whoever had answered the phone.

'Ginny!' exclaimed Alicia, running through to the kitchen in her stockinged feet, shaking the rain from her hair, 'you're up!' She patted delightedly at Ginny's back and shoulders, stuck her finger in the mixing bowl and licked it, said, 'Cake. Spiffing. I'm so happy you're well again,' and waltzed away to hang up her coat. A kind of love welled up in Ginny, sparked simply by the fact that Alicia wasn't Frank. Ginny had her back to the front door and Frank had said nothing, but Ginny knew she was there. The other girl carried an aura for her now, an unwholesomeness that somehow conjured the dank breath of the castle dungeon that would gust up when you walked past it during a northerly.

Their talk that evening was of the Van Heppel Christmas ball. At least, Alicia's was. Frank seemed distracted, almost as if she knew what Ginny had been up to. Surreptitiously, Ginny checked the back of her hand but there was no evidence there now of the number she had called, nothing but a faint red patch where she had scrubbed it off. She had no interest in the ball, she had no intention of going.

'What will you wear, Ginny?' Alicia asked.

'I don't think she's quite with us,' said Frank. 'She's been pretty sick, remember? There's still ages to decide anyway.'

'I'm not going to any ball, Alicia. I'll go and see if the cake's cool enough for icing.'

She could feel their eyes on her back as she went into the kitchen. She had not intended to sound so brusque, but her emotions, it seemed, were out of her control. She split the cake and began to smooth butter icing over the cut surface. By the time she carried it into the sitting room she had managed to fix a smile to her face. She set the cake on the table and cut three slices.

'Scrumptious,' said Alicia, 'we can just have this instead of dinner.' Frank gave an indifferent nod.

'It's just that I don't have the right kind of clothes,' said Ginny, trying to sound conciliatory, 'and I'm not much of a one for parties anyway,' without seeming self-pitying.

'Ginny,' said Alicia, laying the tips of her long fingers gently on Ginny's arm, 'if you want to come to the ball, I can lend you something.'

'It's kind of you, Alicia, but nothing of yours is going to fit me and honestly, I'm completely happy to miss it.'

'But I'd like you to come.'

'Why?'

'The Van Heppels are cousins of mine. I'd account it a favour. I'd like you to meet them, they're awfully nice people.'

Frank suddenly scooted her chair back and reached behind her into the sideboard for the bottle of gin and three glasses, and splashed a generous measure into each.

'Drink up,' she urged, pushing a glass towards Ginny. 'All social events look more alluring through the bottom of a glass.' Ginny's throat narrowed at the prospect but she managed to force down a mouthful and smile her appreciation, uncertain whether to be relieved or on her guard at Frank's abrupt change of mood. As Frank drained her glass, hectic spots of colour appeared in her cheeks and her green eyes glittered like spring leaves in a breeze. 'We should party. Who knows how many more Christmases there'll be?'

'Oh for God's sake, Frank, don't start.' Alicia rose from the table and went upstairs, returning moments later with her arms full of velvet and silk. With a sullen meekness, Frank cleared a space on the table and the gowns spilled out on to it like water. They gave off a faded, floral perfume like falling petals in a deserted room. Ginny estimated there must be at least half a dozen of them and wondered at the life of a girl who owned so many evening dresses, let alone thought it necessary to bring them to this bleak, empty stretch of coast. Maybe, if the Russians figured out what they were doing on the Island and decided to bomb them, Alicia wanted to be confident she could dress for the occasion. Frank had told her once that Alicia's parents had attended the Coronation. Perhaps, among her class of people, there was an etiquette for extinction, something distilled from the Duchess of Richmond's ball on the eve of Waterloo and going over the top at the Somme with nothing to protect you but a cavalry sabre and a well-trimmed moustache.

Alicia picked out a swathe of primrose silk velvet and held it up. It was a full-length gown with a tulip skirt and a short train, and a draped neckline that swooped at the back almost to waist level.

'That would probably just about go round one of my thighs,' Ginny scoffed, taking another slug of gin and feeling a sort of carelessness spread through her.

'Ah, but I have a plan,' said Alicia.

Frank lit a cigarette. 'I love it when Alicia has a plan. God knows, someone has to.'

Alicia extracted another dress from the pile, this one with a full skirt of black lace stiffened by a buckram petticoat. 'This was my mother's,' she said. Oh, thought Ginny, so she thinks I dress like her mother. 'And I've been meaning to do something with it for ages. I mean, no-one would wear that style now unless they were going to a fancy dress do. Totally New Look.'

'So what is the plan?' asked Frank, flicking ash on to her plate among the cake crumbs.

'Aha, you'll have to wait and see. Ginny, let me measure you.' Ginny submitted; the gin made the experience less excruciating than it might have been.

The following morning, as they were about to leave the house for the quay, a knock on the door heralded the postman bearing a telegram for Frank. In Ginny's experience, except for at weddings, telegrams were the harbingers of doom. She hovered, stumble-hearted, as Frank slit the seal and unfolded it, certain it must be connected to yesterday's phone call. What had she been thinking? Neither Frank's life nor Sue's death were any of her business. Sweat broke on her forehead and she wondered if she was sick again; the temptation to flee to her room and crawl back under the covers was momentarily overwhelming.

'Everything OK?' Alicia enquired, and Ginny was relieved because she knew she couldn't trust her own voice. Frank had turned as white as only a redhead could; she looked as if she might faint, her skin bluish. Ginny saw in her mind's eye the image of Sue made by the Artist and thought she was going to be sick.

'Not really,' said Frank. The room swam in front of Ginny's eyes, the mean furniture, the starling sheen of the fire surround, the red Dansette, all swirling as if caught up in a wave. 'My mom is sick.' And then relief, everything settling gently back into its place, and a sharp pang of guilt that her housemate's mother's illness should be cause for relief. 'I have to go to London.'

'Darling, I'm so sorry.' Alicia placed a hand on Frank's arm. 'I'll let the Wingco know for you. I could call you a cab from the Harbourmaster's office if that would help?'

Frank shook her head. 'I'll sort myself out. But thank you,' she added almost as an afterthought, crumpling the telegram in her hand.

'Do give her my best,' Alicia called after her.

Frank was gone for two days. During her absence, the evenings were filled with the whir of Alicia's treadle sewing machine.

'I saw an amazing photo today,' said Ginny, laying out the cards for a game of patience. The photo, glanced at while she was passing Adrian's desk, had moved her unutterably.

'Mmm?' said Alicia, her mouth full of pins.

'A woman sitting on a river bank, mending her kimono. In Hiroshima. There were dead bodies in the river and trees turned to charcoal, and she was just…mending.' The machine paused; the kitchen tap dripped into the silence.

'How lovely,' said Alicia, with a fervency which surprised Ginny. 'Life goes on. We mend.'

'Do you believe in what we're doing?'

'Well, all I do is keep the Wingco's diary really, but I suppose…I think it's a necessary evil. To stop any more wars. Don't you?'

'I'm grateful for the work. If not this, I'd probably be a book-keeper or something. I'm not bored here, and I fit in. In my section at any rate.'

'You will be the belle of the Van Heppel ball once I've finished this.' Alicia smoothed the primrose velvet beneath the sewing machine's foot and pressed the treadle. Ginny returned to her cards. A wind got up later in the evening, rattling the windowpanes and sending a scatter of soot down the chimney. Ginny made cocoa.

They found Frank in the garden when they returned from the Island the next afternoon. She had dragged out one of the dining chairs and was sitting in a slender wedge of evening sunshine. Jazz drifted out through the open door. Frank was engrossed in a book; she didn't look up until Alicia threw a glove at her, though Ginny had the feeling she had been well aware of their approach.

'Hey you, how's Leonora?'

'Hey. Is it that time already?' Frank consulted her watch. 'She's OK. A night in St. Thomas's but they couldn't find a damn thing wrong with her. Ray thought she was having a heart attack. Probably indigestion. Anyway, look what I got! They were queuing outside Foyles almost to Old Compton Street!'

'Lady Chatterley's Lover,' pronounced Alicia, reading the cover as Frank triumphantly brandished the book. 'So, is it as steamy as they say?'

Frank pulled a face. 'I can't say I get what all the fuss was about. I wouldn't mind my wife reading it.' Ginny's insides winced, though she struggled to keep her expression neutral. She had hardly thought of Sue while Frank was away, though she had stayed in her mind as a kind of atmosphere, seeping into Ginny's thoughts and dreams.

'Still,' Frank continued, turning down the corner of her page and closing the book, 'Tout le monde is talking about it so I'd better finish it.'

'I doubt any of the Van Heppel's monde will be, darling.'

Ginny couldn't help a brief smirk.

'But I'll be in London for Christmas, remember, with Mom and Ray.' Ray, who lived with Frank's mother in Chelsea in some not-quite-conventional ménage, was a poet and, according to Frank, an advocate of free love. Was that what they were defending, Ginny wondered. Free love?

'So what will you say when tout le monde asks your opinion?' she asked Frank, her mockery sounding to her own ears brittle and unconvincing, but Frank did not seem to notice anything amiss.

'That it's not about love at all, it's about power. It

reduces Lady Chatterley to some poor creature who can't function without regular orgasms and furthermore implies only a man can provide her with what she needs. What about masturbation, what about…?'

'Frank, please, we're not in Ray's studio now. You're embarrassing Ginny.' Alicia unlocked the door and stepped inside. Ginny followed her.

'Well she shouldn't be embarrassed,' Frank called after them. 'We should be thinking about the power of our bodies and how to reclaim it. Look at us! We dress for men, we take their names, we give them babies to continue their line. Simone de Beauvoir was exactly right. We're doomed to passivity and we just have to wait for some magic to happen to get us what we want.'

'And for D. H. Lawrence that magic is a horny game-keeper?' Alicia called back.

'I know! Ridiculous! All body, no brain.'

Ginny wished they would keep their voices down. They were oblivious, talking about girls like themselves, attractive, privileged girls who might plausibly expect magic to happen. Ginny had never had any expectation of magic in her own life, yet even as she thought this, a voice in her head which was not her own asked, what about the maths, isn't that some kind of magic, my lunar girl?

'If this…Simone de…?'

'Beauvoir,' said Alicia, kindly.

'If she knew all this, why didn't she do something about it?'

'What do you mean?' Alicia's lovely face knit itself in puzzlement.

'She did,' said Frank, following them into the house. 'She wrote The Second Sex.'

'The second sex,' Ginny repeated. 'That rather suggests accepting the status quo, don't you think? Two. The oddest prime. One, on the other hand, represents a single entity. Whatever you multiply by one stays the same. It's its own factorial, square, square root, cube, cube root…'

'Enough!' Frank shouted, holding her hands in the air like a surrendering cowboy. 'What's your point?'

'Just that if she'd called her book The First Sex, it might have been, I don't know, more of a statement of intent.'

'I think,' said Frank, looking at Ginny as if she had been overtaken by an involuntary admiration, 'you might just have a point there. And,' she flung Lady Chatterley's Lover onto the sagging settee, 'why Lady Chatterley's lover? Like he's the main focus here, not her. I'll tell you why.'

'Why, darling?' asked Alicia.

'Because it was written by a man, that's why. What does he know about our bodies, our feelings?'

Ginny busied herself taking off her outdoor clothes and tried to quell the fierce flush that was creeping up her neck. Alicia stood with her scarf half unwound, one shoe on, one off, her violet eyes misted like storm clouds. 'I like to think there's at least one man, somewhere, who'll understand my body…or learn to,' she added wistfully.

'Dumb romantic.' Frank headed for the kitchen. 'What's to eat?'

Alicia made omelettes and afterwards announced, 'I think our Cinderella computer's ballgown is ready for a fitting. Frank, you can give us an impartial assessment.'

'Hmmm.' Frank was going through the day's post. Whatever she was hoping for wasn't there, it seemed. 'Just bills.'

'Leave them out,' said Alicia. 'I'll take them to Bonn in the morning.' Frank gave a wolf whistle. Poor Bonn, thought Ginny. Simone de Beauvoir was wrong that only girls had to wait for magic to happen.

Up in Alicia's room after dinner, among dust devils and swags of beads and scarves draped over every surface and that same scent of dying flowers, Ginny stripped to her underwear and allowed Alicia to help her into the dress. Alicia shifted a handful of scarves and necklaces from the cheval glass, the only full-length mirror in the house, and pushed Ginny in front of it. Her obvious excitement made her a little rough. Ginny looked at herself.

Alicia had shortened the yellow velvet to just below the knee and simplified the neckline, and used the spare fabric to insert gores in the skirt which flattered what Ginny's mother called her 'pear shape'. She had used the black lace from her mother's dress to fill in the scooped back and create little capped sleeves. As a finishing touch she had created a sash from a length of black Petersham ribbon.

'Don't mind Frank,' said Alicia, standing behind Ginny so their eyes met in the mirror. 'She just hates it when she isn't the centre of attention.'

'I supposes she misses Sue.'

Alicia took a step back. 'Why do you say that?'

'I had the impression they were close.'

'Not especially. She was upset, of course, we all were. It was a terrible shock, just terrible.' She shivered, her pale reflection blurring behind Ginny's shoulder.

'Bonn pointed out to me where she'd been swimming. It looks a dangerous spot. She must have been quite a swimmer to attempt it.' In the photograph, Sue had looked to have strong shoulders, though her bones were fine, light, easily caught up in a current and swept away.

'I suppose so,' said Alicia, and began to fuss with the dress, pinching and straightening seams, smoothing the skirt.

'You've made this really lovely,' said Ginny. She could not pursue the conversation about Sue without revealing she had seen that photo, but something did not sit right, she was sure of it. She forced her attention back to the dress, which was indeed lovely. She would never have chosen such an impractical colour for herself but she had to admit it suited her skin, brought out a glow in it she had not known was there. And the gored skirt did flatter her figure.

'All you need now is shoes, and a hair do. Why don't you and I go up to town on Saturday? We can't let Frank have all the fun. We could have tea at Fortnums and look at the Christmas lights on Regent Street.'

'Alright.' She could forego the hairdresser and decline cakes at Fortnums on the grounds of needing to keep slim for the dress, and there was a Freeman Hardy Willis on Oxford Street or thereabouts, she thought, where she could find shoes that were both cheap and sensible. So really it would just be the price of a train ticket and a pot of tea. And it would be a fine treat to see the lights.

She crossed the landing to her own room to change, though she did take up Alicia's offer of a padded coathanger with a lavender bag for the dress. Her curtains were still open and she paused before drawing them to look at the castle, silhouetted against a gibbous moon whose face was periodically veiled by skeins of flying, silver-edged cloud. She caught movement out of the tail of her eye, a glimmer of something close to the steps that led down to the dungeons. Some night creature, perhaps, or tufts of wool snagged on the fence that barred access to the steps, now crumbled with age and dangerous.

There came a knock on the door, but before she could answer it, Frank barged into the room, closed the door quietly behind her and leaned against it. Her eyes glittered dangerously in the fitful moonlight. Ginny's heart began to thud heavily in her chest. Was Frank making her a prisoner? She broke out in a sweat and wished she had had time to take off the dress before she spoiled it.

'You've been poking your nose into things that are none of your business,' Frank hissed.

'Please, Frank, I want to get changed.' She drew in a deep breath, tried to stop her voice from shaking and whining as if she was a kicked puppy. 'I'm sorry. You're right, I had no business phoning Sue's parents like that. I didn't plan to...I was just...I wanted to know what had happened to her. It was something the Artist said.'

'The Artist?' For a second Frank looked strangely afraid, then her expression cleared and she began to laugh, a harsh, cruel sound. 'I'm not sure I even believe in your artist. I mean, I've never seen him, nor has Alicia, and who the hell would want to paint you anyway?'

'Did you kill her, Frank? Did...the things you did to her drive her to drown herself? I've seen the place where it happened. No-one would choose to go swimming there. The cross-currents are far too dangerous.'

'The things I did to her,' Frank repeated, sauntering away from the door and sitting on Ginny's bed. 'The things I did to her? You're a stupid girl, Ginny, a stupid, bigoted, narrow-minded girl and you've put me in a very difficult position with your blundering curiosity.'

'She did die because of you! I knew it!'

'For the record,' said Frank, rising from the bed and approaching the door, where she turned towards Ginny with her hand resting on the door knob, 'although the Coroner recorded a verdict of accidental death, I think it's quite possible Sue didn't make much effort to save herself. She was a troubled person, weak, always trying to be someone she wasn't. But I didn't kill her. Perhaps all of us did, with our prejudices and our prickly morals. She was thin-skinned and we tore her to shreds.' There was a catch in her voice and tears in her eyes, but when Ginny reached out a comforting hand towards her she shied away and seemed to steel herself. 'And also for the record,' she went on, 'that number you rang didn't belong to Sue's parents, and if you rang it again you'd find it was dead.' She left, closing the door behind her with ominous care.

# 8

On the evening of the ball, Frank announced that she was going to do Ginny's makeup. She had been as nice as pie to Ginny since their argument about Sue, often sitting with her in the canteen at lunchtime and showing an interest in Ginny's work which she had never done before. She even told Alicia to put the Fortnums cream teas on her mother's account when she and Ginny went up to London shoe-shopping, though she declined their invitation to join them.

'I hope your mother's feeling better,' Ginny had said.

'Oh, she's fine,' Frank replied breezily, 'she's indestructible. She could probably have walked out of Hiroshima without a scratch on her.' Ginny thought her remark in excruciating taste, but it would have been impolite to say so when Frank was buying her tea. Besides, she was probably being oversensitive. Too much exposure to Adrian's photographs.

Before makeup, however, they were all going to lie on

their beds for twenty minutes with slices of cucumber over their eyes. Alicia had spent a small fortune on a hothouse cucumber for this very purpose. The ritual complete, Frank summoned Ginny to her room, where she had not set foot since her discovery of the photograph. It felt odd to walk in there, to be ushered to the dressing table and to sit in front of the mirror where the family snap seemed to be the one bright spot. It was already pitch-dark outside and the room was dingily lit by a single overhead bulb and a bedside table lamp which Frank now carried over to the dressing table to light Ginny's face while she worked. Ginny looked at herself in dismay; the lamp gave her skin a jaundiced cast and accentuated the lopsidedness of her nose, a consequence, her mother said darkly, of a difficult birth.

Outside, snow had begun to fall. Whenever Frank tipped her face towards the window, Ginny observed its progress, from freckling to coating the ground, evening out potholes in the pub yard much as Frank's powders and paints were gradually smoothing out the imperfections of her face. She had to admit, Frank was good at this. When the final sweep of lipstick and pother of powder had been applied, the reflection in the mirror gave Ginny genuine pleasure. She looked…well…sophisticated, her brows shaped and pencilled, her eyes outlined in black, with a tiny upward flick at the corners, her cheekbones highlighted with rouge. What must Frank really think of her, she wondered, to be able to make her look like this?

On an impulse, when she had put on the black and primrose dress, she took out Sue's pendant from the back of the drawer where she had hidden it behind a box of Dr. Whites and fastened it around her neck. She picked up the hagstone from her dressing table and looked at her reflection through the hole. The pearl sat neatly in the hollow between her collarbones and glowed like a tiny moon at her throat. She fancied she could feel a warmth emanating from it. She meant to take it off again before going downstairs, but before she could, Frank walked in behind a perfunctory knock, bearing a bottle of Je Reviens.

'I thought...' she began, and stopped, her knuckles whitening around the perfume bottle until Ginny feared she would break it, her face drained of colour.

'Where did you find that?' Frank's voice had something ancient about it, low and hoarse, a sort of lupine growl. There was clearly no point in Ginny trying to pass the necklace off as her own.

'I found it. On the floor behind the dressing table.'

'Why didn't you say anything?'

'What was there to say?'

'It could have been mine, or Alicia's.'

'I knew it wasn't.' Outside, the snow continued to fall. She found herself thinking about the Artist, and how cold his hands must be, how strangely cold the pearl burned at her throat. Weren't pearls supposed to be warm to the touch?

'So you stole it. Deliberately?'

'I don't think you can steal from the dead.'

She could see Frank hesitating in the doorway, felt herself, by contrast, stone-still, her face a mask. Then Frank gave a brief, resigned smile and said,

'Well, do you want a dab of this or not?' Ginny held out her wrists. As Frank dotted them with perfume, the girls' eyes met, held for a moment. Ginny fancied dark specks swam in the green of Frank's irises, like seals' heads in the sea.

'Taxi's here!' called Alicia from the bottom of the stairs. From time to time, in the future, the moment would come back to Ginny and she was never certain which of them broke eye contact first or what might have been said if the taxi had arrived a minute later.

\*

They should have taken the jeep, she thought, as the taxi skidded and slithered along the narrow lanes, the wind lifting flurries of snow from the stubble fields and hurrying it across their path. It might be open-sided, with the suspension of a cart, but it would have suited the weather better, and it would have got them there on time.

'We're so late now they'll think us downright rude,' snapped Alicia as the taxi driver slid to a halt in front of a snow drift and began to back up in search of an alternative route.

'Still bordering on fashionable,' consoled Frank, taking a swig from her hip flask and offering it to Alicia. Alicia turned away and hunched deeper into her mink. Ginny, in her gabardine, envied Alicia her furs; the taxi's heater seemed to have no effect but to push dust around the stale tobacco-smelling air.

'Maybe for your Chelsea Arts set,' Alicia muttered.

'God, don't be so provincial!'

'The Van Heppels are provincial.'

As an ill-tempered silence descended, the driver, with a triumphant, 'Here it be,' yanked the wheel suddenly to the left and the cab tacked between imposing gateposts, miraculously avoiding hitting either. The gryphons atop each were wearing comical snow cone hats. The driveway ahead of them was marked out by flambeaux, haloes of sparkling snow, the shadows of trees and bushes reaching across an expanse of whitened lawn towards Aldeford Manor.

It was not a grand house, Ginny realised as they drew up at the door, but long and low beneath a thatched roof, the light from its many windows falling fragmented through a myriad tiny leaded panes. Tall barley twist chimneys reached up into the night sky gnarled as witches' fingers. A small flight of worn stone steps led to a doorway set deep within a brick arch. There they were met by a housekeeper in black bombazine who took their coats and directed them across a broad hall towards open double doors from which light and music and a hubbub of voices spilled. The hall was roof height, with a gallery running around it at first floor level. At the foot of the stairs was a Christmas tree that must have been twenty feet tall, festooned with tinsel and real candles. The scent of charred pine mingled with that of beeswax polish and mulled wine.

Once she had discarded her gabardine, Ginny felt as though she had sloughed off an old skin. As she crossed the hall, it no longer seemed to matter that her new patent slingbacks pinched her toes. The rustle of her lace and velvet dress seemed to whisper that she was beautiful, desirable, a young woman come into the fullness of herself. She moved with confidence towards the receiving line where Alicia, a swan in yards of cream silk tulle, introduced her to a stoutish woman in green satin, her iron-grey hair imperfectly restrained in a bun by a set of tortoiseshell and marcasite combs.

'Miss Matlock,' boomed the woman, 'delighted to meet you. My husband, Maurice.' A tall man as slender as his wife was stout, with an attentive stoop which gave him the air of a slightly deaf professor. His cuffs a little frayed. 'I suppose you work on the base too, do you?' the woman continued, clearly confident her husband would have nothing to say. 'Alicia's been here for two years, you know, and not a husband in sight. I keep telling Drum – Wing Commander Drummond – I say, Drum, she's too good for you, she ought to be up in town. Hiding her light under a bushel here, she is.'

'Darling Aunt Ronnie, we have this conversation at least twice a year. I like it here. I feel useful. If I was looking for a husband I'd probably go to Saudi Arabia and bag myself a sheikh so Daddy could repair the roof at Marlings.'

'Really, Alicia. What do you do, Miss Matlock? Secretarial as well, I suppose?'

'Ginny,' said Frank, stepping forward to shake hands with the Van Heppels, 'is a computer.'

'Good heavens! Did you hear that, Maurice? A female computer. Well I never. How very modern.'

Ginny crashed back to earth. Suddenly, she was certain everyone would know that her dress was Alicia's cast-off and her shoes were leatherette. Everyone would know the pearl at her throat belonged to a dead girl. She was an imposter, a misfit, not a real girl but some awful sort of hybrid, like Frankenstein's monster. She moved down the receiving line, nodding and smiling, wondering if she would be able to find somewhere quiet to hide until their cab returned to take them home, tempted to jab one of her kitten heels into Frank's foot.

'I think it's marvellous,' chimed in the young man at the end of the line, holding out his hand. He stood partly in shadow and she had not noticed him until now. His voice was arresting, pitched so Ginny could hear him perfectly above the hubbub in the room yet hoarse, as if he was suffering from a mild sore throat. 'Awfully brave.' His grip was firm and dry and somehow matched his voice. Brave struck her as an odd choice of word, but also one she wanted to live up to. As the young man released her hand and turned to Frank with some joke or other, she stepped into the room.

The furniture had been pushed back against the walls and a dais rigged up in front of a cavernous fireplace where a jazz trio was playing softly, or perhaps it was just that the music was lost in the recesses of the chimney. Guests were clumped together in small groups and waiters whirled between them with trays of champagne cocktails and canapés. Occasional gusts of hearty laughter afforded the band even more competition. She recognised Adrian and his wife stranded at the edge of the room between a dark red Chesterfield and a stack of dining chairs. With their young host's description of her as brave still echoing somewhere in her chest cavity, Ginny made her way to join them, taking a glass from one of the waiters en route. Adrian's wife, she thought, looked nice, her comfortable curves swathed in royal blue rayon, her good-natured face lightly powdered. The hand clutching her glass was broad and strong, with small, pink-frosted nails. It made Ginny glad to see her because she didn't think Adrian could do the job he did, day after day poring over those awful photos from Hiroshima and Nagasaki, if his home life were anything other than unexceptional. Mrs. Fletcher struck her as the embodiment of what it was they were all there to protect. She provoked neither fatal pessimism nor irony. She radiated a steady ordinariness in which Ginny basked as they chatted, about the snow and how much the children loved it, and plans for Christmas, and what exactly that creamy, salmon pink substance in the vol-au-vents might be. Not salmon, that was for certain. She thought she might stay beside Mrs. Fletcher all evening, but then the jazz trio was joined by more musicians and the dancing began, and Bonn, resplendent in his mess kit, appeared in front of her, bowing and clicking his heels and asking her to dance. Had Alicia rejected him again, Ginny wondered, feeling obliged to accept?

She was not a very good dancer, but in Mrs. Fletcher's magnanimous glow this did not seem to matter. And Bonn was accomplished, leading her with grace and authority through a foxtrot and a quickstep, guiding her among the other couples on the floor as if following a path laid out especially for the two of them. A waltz struck up. Ginny and Bonn took a couple of turns and then everything unravelled. As Bonn whirled her past the dark red Chesterfield, and she looked out for Mrs. Fletcher, she noticed two people seated there, so deep in conversation their heads were almost touching. Frank, and the Artist, in whom Frank did not, apparently, believe. Ginny stumbled to a halt, although it felt as if her head was still spinning, everything around her blurred except the two figures on the Chesterfield. Fire and water.

'Oh dear, Ginny, are you quite alright? Was it my fault? Did I trip you?' Bonn helped her to her feet. Her stocking was torn and she had a splinter in her right knee. She was not in pain, but tears threatened nonetheless because the dream of Mrs. Fletcher had been punctured. Bonn led her towards the Chesterfield. She tried to protest that she had no need to sit down but he was insistent. She must rest. He would bring her a drink. He steered her firmly towards the Chesterfield, where she could put up her leg and he could take a look at the damage.

'But…' Could he not see Frank and the Artist there?

'But nothing, Miss Ginny Matlock. You're not in Section Four now. I'm in charge. And here's Frank to keep an eye on you until I return bearing champagne and sticking plasters. All on your ownsome, Frankie? '

'Just taking a breather.' Frank shuffled along the seat to make room for Ginny. Where was the Artist, she wondered, sitting down cautiously, irrationally fearful of finding herself in the Artist's lap?

'Here,' said Frank, patting her knees. 'Put your foot up. It'll help stop the bleeding and save your dress from getting ruined. Lord knows how we'd explain bloodstains to Alicia.' Bonn cleared his throat. 'Don't worry, Bonn, or maybe do. She's danced at least three numbers with Dom.' Ginny thought of Alicia's bitten nails and a sudden, inexpressible sadness washed over her. As soon as Bonn went off in search of Dettol and tweezers, she turned to Frank and asked,

'Where is he?'

'Who?'

'You know perfectly well who I mean. The Artist. I saw you talking to him. You can't keep pretending you don't know who he is.'

'Ginny, Ginny, did you hit your head when you fell? There's no-one here but me. Like I said, taking a moment. This ballroom stuff is so boring.' More likely, Ginny thought, Frank just didn't like dancing with men.

'I don't understand the big mystery. Why pretend you don't know him when you clearly do?'

'Ginny, I don't. I don't know anyone who looks the way your describe him. I would surely remember someone so striking.' She looked around the room with an exaggerated craning of her neck. 'And he would certainly stand out in this crowd, yet I don't see him. Do you?'

Ginny didn't reply. What was the point? Without waiting for Bonn, she put her shoes back on and limped out through the French windows, which gave on to a stone terrace overlooking the gardens.

It had stopped snowing, but the temperature had dropped with the clearing of the cloud cover. Flambeaux burned along the balustrade and flanked steps leading to the lawn, but beyond their flicker and glow the garden lapsed into darkness, only a rime of starlight outlining the mounds of snow-mantled shrubbery. Someone closed the doors behind her and suddenly the party seemed very far away. Footsteps approached along the terrace, ringing in the frosty air.

'Miss Matlock?' An American accent, something deep and cowboyish that conjured leather chaps, painted ponies and red, wind-sculpted rocks.

'Yes?' Though when she turned to look at the man, she saw he was in evening dress and a long way off the looks of Gary Cooper or James Stewart.

'Larry McGuire.' He held out his hand. 'I've been wanting to make your acquaintance.' They shook; his grip was firm, but cold and slightly damp, as if he had just put down an iced drink. Which perhaps he had. 'You bunk with Frank Tettridge, don't you?'

Suddenly, Ginny was on her guard. Perhaps his remark was no more than an innocent conversation opener but there was a plain pointedness to it that made her think otherwise.

'I do.' She decided not to say any more until Mr. Larry McGuire made the purpose of his question clearer. It was a poor chat-up line on so many levels she felt no inclination to help him along anyway.

'Tell me about her.' He was trying so hard to sound casual that Ginny almost took pity on him.

'I wonder what exactly you want to know, Mr. McGuire?'

'Larry, please.' She did not rise to his bait. He cleared his throat. 'We're…concerned about her,' he said.

'Who is "we"?'

'Her work colleagues, in the USAF liaison office. We think she may be…keeping inadvisable company.' Ginny's mind flew to the image of Frank and the Artist together on the Chesterfield. Her heart set up a sick thudding in her chest.

'You mean the Artist?'

A puzzled frown knit itself between his brows. 'I'm not familiar with anyone goes by that name,' he said.

'I don't know much – anything – about him really, but he's here somewhere. I saw him and Frank talking together earlier. A very striking man, with long hair. And Frank denied point-blank knowing him.'

'A beatnik, you mean?' Hope flickered in the depths of Larry McGuire's narrow, pale eyes.

'Oh no, not at all. More like…' She trawled her memory for an appropriate image and came up with, 'Dürer. I think that's his name.'

'The painter?'

She gave a weak smile. 'Appropriately enough.'

McGuire looked disappointed. 'I don't think we're familiar with anyone fitting that description. Could you point him out to us?'

'You'll know him if you see him. As I said, he's very distinctive.'

'Of course. You have been most helpful already, and I have kept you away from your friends for too long. But we will speak again, Miss Matlock.' A man of remorseless patience.

'Will we?'

He left her feeling rattled and agitated; he had manipulated her somehow, but she could not grasp how or to what end? Should she have mentioned glimpsing Frank out by the pagodas that time, on the day of the big storm? Should she have mentioned Sue? She wrestled with herself briefly over these questions but in the end concluded she had been right not to volunteer any more information. She had no idea who Larry McGuire was, and only his word that he worked with Frank. She could not recall ever seeing him on the base or around the village. Yet she already knew she would say nothing to Frank about her conversation with him.

As the French window closed behind him the cold silence washed back in like a cleansing wave. She breathed it deep into her lungs, into the very tips of her fingers and pinched toes, into the mild throbbing of her knee and the constraint of her girdle, into the roots of her hair as they stirred to prevent the escape of her body heat. She wondered if her eyes might freeze if she didn't blink, yet the view, monochromatic and pared of detail, was so mesmerically serene she could not bear to shut it out even for a second. If she did not keep looking, it might disappear altogether.

'When I was a little boy, I had a copy of Hans Christian Andersen's The Snow Queen with illustrations just like this. I loved that story, perhaps there's a sliver of Kai in me, and every time I turned a page, I used to believe the illustration I could no longer see had melted. Every time I came back to the story, it seemed to have made itself anew.'

The voice sounded familiar, but it was not the Artist, not McGuire nor any of the other men she knew from the base. Steps approached her from further along the terrace and, when the speaker moved into the guttering light cast by one of the flambeaux, she recognised the young man from the end of the receiving line. What was his name? Had he told her? The beginning of the evening seemed an age ago.

'Philip Van Heppel,' he said. He drew a silver cigarette case from his inside breast pocket and offered it to her. She took a cigarette and put it to her lips, noting its oval shape and the rich, floral aroma it gave off when Philip Van Heppel lit it and she inhaled. Sullivan and Powell's Turkish; Alicia always brought a stock back with her when she went up to London. They were strong, unfiltered, and made Ginny a little dizzy.

'Did you never wonder why the pages didn't get wet?' The half of Philip's face which was not in shadow looked puzzled. 'From the melting snow?'

'Aha, the logic of the computer.' He smiled. She noticed how a bracket appeared at the corner of his mouth, as if his smiles were something he kept in parenthesis. 'No, I didn't. I must have been a fanciful child, I suppose. And you? Quadratic equations at five? Times crossword at seven? No cloud cover in your brain, I expect.'

'And now?' she enquired, choosing not to answer him because she thought his questions sounded patronising.

'Oh…now…' When he failed to elaborate she turned away from the view of the garden, which she had been contemplating with her arms resting on the balustrade, to look at him. He had moved closer to her, she realised; running through the fragrance of the Turkish tobacco was something sharper, sweat, an expensive cologne with a citrusy note. Her body seemed to be relaxing into his closeness, her skin warmed, her heartbeat thick and slow in her chest, yet her mind remained wary, pulsing out warning signals which seemed to get lost in the atmosphere, as often happened at the communications station on the base when there was heavy cloud, or the wind was in the wrong direction, confounding the radio waves, garbling the fragile strings of code.

The skin on the right side of his face, which had been hidden from her until now, was as taut and shiny as an over-inflated balloon, except where his ear should have been, where it was puckered around a featureless lump of gristle. A melted ear, she found herself thinking as her attention shifted over the polished bone of his cheek and hairless brow. He was no longer smiling, but his gaze remained steadily on her, one blue eye fringed by thick, fair lashes and one peering out from a tear in the shiny skin. She found herself trying so hard to keep a neutral expression her teeth were clamped together, her tongue pushed into the back of them as if to stop them chattering.

'Well,' he said, 'things changed. As you can see.' She nodded; she felt as useful as one of those nodding dogs people put in the rear windows of their cars.

'I'm sorry. I didn't mean to upset you. It's just that… I couldn't help overhearing some of your conversation with that unpleasant Yank and had some chivalrous notion of rescuing you. Silly of me. Please forget about it.'

She hadn't succeeded at all in hiding her revulsion, had she? 'No! I'm sorry, I didn't mean…please, finish what you were going to say. Tell me what happened, I want to know.' She forced her gaze to connect with his, her mouth to smile. She was gripping her cigarette so hard between her index and middle fingers it had squeezed flat and strands of tobacco were drifting out of the end of it on to the snowy terrace. Philip leaned forward, took it from her and ground it out under his foot, and offered her a fresh one from the case. For a second of panic, she thought her hand would refuse to obey her and take the cigarette, but it did, and Philip lit it, careful not to lean too close to her, the space between them charged. Philip took a deep drag on his own cigarette and continued,

'I was watching you dance earlier. For some reason it made me think you wouldn't feel the things most girls feel. Revulsion, fear, disappointment.' He gave a short, bitter laugh. 'I'd be quite a catch, you know, without this.' He waved his free hand vaguely at his face. 'Mrs. Bennett would be inviting me to dine at every end and turn.'

'You thought, I suppose,' Ginny retorted, 'that being a computer, and a poor dancer to boot, I wouldn't feel much. Please…don't insult me by denying it. It's what everyone thinks, even if they don't say it. A female computer is downright unnatural.' She glared at him, half wondering if she was waiting for him to contradict her.

'That makes two of us, then,' he said quietly, holding her gaze. His eyes, she noticed in the guttering beams of the flambeaux, were really rather beautiful, their grey-blue irises flecked with amber around the pupils. A smile found its way on to her face, stretching out its tense muscles.

'Though I'm certainly not proposing we do anything unnatural together.' The lopsidedness conferred on his grin by his injury gave it a rakish air. His teeth seemed very white, perhaps because the uninjured half of his face was weathered and ruddy. 'But we could dance?'

'I really don't enjoy it, if you don't mind.'

'Thank you for your honesty.' He made a shallow bow, as if taking his leave.

'I only meant that I don't like to dance. I would enjoy staying out here a little longer, it's so beautiful now the sky's cleared.' They both looked up at the luminous smear of the Milky Way. 'Would you tell me what happened to you?'

'Not much to tell. Korea. Fleet Air Arm. I was trying to land in filthy weather in the South China Sea and missed the deck of the carrier. Seems odd that anything should catch fire in the water, but it's the fuel. Just floats there on the top and burns. I imagine you probably know the science of it better than I do. Anyway, I got out in better nick than the aircraft, poor old girl.'

Fire and water.

Images from Adrian's photos drifted across her mind like ashes. 'Did you hear everything the American was saying?'

'No, hardly any of it. I just didn't like his demeanour. He seemed overbearing, even if he is built like a lab rat.'

'That's good,' said Ginny, 'that's exactly right.' If your own appearance was botched, she wondered, did that cause you to be abnormally astute in assessing other peoples'? 'Were you in hospital a long time?'

'Quite a few months. And now, just like Cincinnatus, I've come back to the home farm.'

'I'm afraid I went to grammar school. The only Greek I know is pi.'

The lopsided grin reappeared. 'That's a decent joke, even if Cincinnatus was a Roman.'

'Oh dear.'

'I'm sure pi is more useful than the legend of Cincinnatus in our modern world.'

'So do you actually farm or do you have a manager?'

'Oh, I farm. I'm the manager for my father, I suppose. We only have about six hundred acres, not really enough to justify a manager. Mixed arable and livestock. Mainly beef cattle, some sheep. I expect you'd find it very boring after the excitements of the base.'

She thought she would like farming, the predictability of the seasons and their rituals, the rows of crops, the accounting for weights and measures and square yards. 'The trouble with our cutting edge,' she said, 'is that you don't always know where it is. The more detailed the calculations, the more uncertain the outcomes. People don't understand that about maths.'

'Strikes me the Island is an ideal place for you to be. You know it's only been there about three hundred years? My ancestors in this house would have got up one morning after a storm and found their coastline completely shifted about. Land where there was water and water where there was land. I try to think about that sometimes, wonder how they felt, what they believed. I imagine them leading the villagers into Saint Jude's and the parish priest, who might not have had much education, casting about for a way of explaining it to them, of reassuring them. Our communities are so fragile, so easily turned on their heads.'

'How do you think he might have explained the legend of the merman?' In her mind's eye she saw the crucified Christ on the lady chapel wall, the pale locks coiled over his dislocated shoulders.

'Ah, the merman. Well, before the Reformation I like to think he would have had his place in our local martyrology. After that I expect he became the Work of the Devil, don't you? The Reformation doesn't seem to have done much for either our imagination or our tolerance, a situation now nicely rectified by the landlords of the pub. Which, as it happens, is us.' He gave a self-satisfied smile. She liked his neat summary, which conferred a measure of containment on the legend and made it feel safe.

'I hate those prints, though. Sorry.'

'Don't be. I hate them too but they were our tenant's choice. Apparently the tourists appreciate them, and they help him sell those little booklets he keeps in the bar. Half a crown each he charges! Makes me wonder if we shouldn't put up his rent.'

'I hadn't noticed them, but I don't like to go in there, if I'm honest. There's an atmosphere…'

'I shall put that down to your finely-tuned brain. Never noticed it myself but then, I've been going in there for so long. Tenant bought me my first legal drink! Perhaps I'm immune to the merman and all his wiles.' Ginny hoped fervently that he was.

Just then she heard someone clear their throat and the Artist came into view only feet away from her, his pallor incandescent in a sudden flare of torchlight, his eyes glimmering in dark sockets. He leaned on a cane and she realised she had never before seen him standing. His legs were short in relation to his body to the point of deformity and seemed to curve at the knee more than bend, as if the joints were soft. She wondered if he had suffered from rickets as a child; a lot did, who had grown up in the war. War disfigured.

'Lovely evening now,' she remarked, but the Artist made no reply other than to flash her an odd, knowing smile before starting painfully down the steps towards the lawn. Probably looking for somewhere to hide from McGuire, she thought.

'An altogether safer subject of conversation,' said Philip with light irony, glancing up at the sky. 'Not even a bomber's moon. Cold, though. Look at you, you're shivering.'

She had been watching the Artist. It was only once he was lost to the shadows of the garden beyond the light of the flambeaux that her attention returned to Philip.

'Let me take you in to supper,' he said, removing his jacket and placing it around her shoulders.

'Alright,' she agreed, casting one last glance over the pristine sparkle of the snow-shrouded garden. It was not until Philip had shepherded her to a seat and gone to fill their plates at the buffet that the realisation came to her. There had been no footsteps on the lawn, no trace at all of the Artist in the pristine snow.

But then Philip returned with supper and more champagne, and after supper, Frank set up the radiogram and stacked the turntable with records she had brought with her: Buddy Holly, Elvis Presley, the Four Tops. The older generation took their leave or retreated to another room and the young took over the dance floor. They did the Twist, the Pony, the Shimmy, the new dances that allowed them to move in shifting, syncopated groups rather than couples, yet Philip stayed near Ginny, and she noticed he moved well. Farming, she supposed, kept you fit. By the time the party finally drifted to a close around four in the morning, and he wondered if she would like to meet up for a trip to the cinema once Christmas was out of the way, she was ready to agree without hesitation.

'So,' said Alicia, as soon as they were settled in the taxi for the slow journey home. She was grinning like the Cheshire Cat. 'Cousin Philip?'

'What about him?'

'So disingenuous,' said Frank, over her shoulder from

the front where she sat hugging her pile of records. 'The Russians'd never get a thing out of you.'

'You were out on the terrace for ages,' Alicia continued, 'and he was making cow eyes at you all through supper. And I swear I overheard something about the cinema...?'

'You must have been awfully bored if you had nothing better to do than keep an eye on me and Philip. Was that exotic-looking chap in the cummerbund so much less fascinating than he seemed?'

Frank snorted. 'Dominic Blythe-Tripp,' she announced. 'He's been pursuing Alicia for years.'

'The trouble is,' said Alicia, 'he never quite takes his eye off himself so he can focus on the prize. Now, Philip. He's an absolute sweetheart but girls are always letting him down. You won't do that, will you, Ginny?'

'Well, it's not as if an invitation to the cinema after Christmas is a proposal of marriage exactly. It'll probably never happen anyway. But if you mean his face...' She paused, to examine her feelings and find the words to fit them. 'I liked him. If you like a person, you like their face.' She stopped, briefly overwhelmed by the hope that he felt the same about her face and that the cinema trip would indeed happen. Alicia reached across the seat to squeeze Ginny's hand and Ginny was afraid she might cry; it was the first time either of the girls had displayed anything more towards her than the cheerful tolerance of housemates thrown together by circumstance rather than choice.

They travelled on without conversation, Alicia dozing with her head on Ginny's shoulder, Frank giving occasional directions to the cabbie. Ginny wished she could doze off too, but she couldn't.

'Frank?' she asked eventually, 'who's Larry McGuire?'

After an almost imperceptible hesitation, like those

jumps that sometimes happened in the cinema when the film had been imperfectly spliced, Frank laughed and said,

'God! He wasn't trying to hit on you too, was he? What an exciting night you've had, Ginny. He's just a guy in the office, one of the civilians, if you know what I mean.'

'I'm not sure I do.'

'The intelligence guys.' She turned to face Ginny, her eyes wide in mock terror. 'The CIA.' Ginny's heart lurched. Her reaction must have shown on her face because Frank laughed again. 'He's a paper-pusher, hun. The only thing he knows how to do with a gun is make up a requisition for it in triplicate.'

Either Frank was dumber than she looked, Ginny concluded, or she thought Ginny was. She decided it was best to say no more until she knew which it was. She let her mind drift back to Philip van Heppel.

# 9

He took her to see A Breath of Scandal at the Odeon in Ipswich. The film was ridiculous and the heating in the cinema had broken down. They sat stiffly, side by side, strangers, almost, among couples who clearly knew one another a lot better and had their own ways of keeping warm. Ginny thought her embarrassment might be able to generate enough energy to heat the place, and tried to pass the time by devising an equation for its specific thermal capacity. To her astonishment, under the influence of a warming scotch in the cheerful fug of a pub they just managed to slip into before last orders, she confessed to Philip what she had been thinking about as Sophia Loren pouted and Maurice Chevalier tried to look angry and John Gavin did a good impression of a tailor's dummy. The second the words were out of her mouth she regretted them; he would think her unfeminine, unhinged, probably. And certainly ungrateful.

He started to laugh. Mortified, Ginny felt her cheeks begin to burn. He was laughing in a way which drew attention to them, which unsettled her because she had noticed how he kept his face in the shadow of a broad-brimmed fedora until they were seated in the dark cinema.

'I know I'm not very romantic,' she began. 'I've not been on that many dates…' There had been two, three if you included Jimmy Ferris who lived next door and who had taken her out skating one winter because his mother asked him to. One had been entirely boring, the other both boring and frightening, when the boy in question took her round the back of the dance hall 'for a smoke' and turned out to have something very much else in mind. She didn't like to think what would have happened if the night watchman for the bank next door hadn't come along when he did.

'Stop!' gasped Philip. 'Ginny, stop it. I'm not laughing at you, I'm laughing at us. I have to confess I was mostly wondering what my Angus bullocks would fetch at auction next week. I've been grazing them on salt grass, wondered if it might improve the flavour.'

For a few seconds Ginny thought she should behave as if he had insulted her, but then something inside her began to open up, like a clenched fist relaxing. They were not playing games, she realised, not acting out any script Alicia or Frank might have written for them. Her unconscious had prompted her before she was even aware of it that she could be herself with Philip, and he could be himself with her.

'Which is actually a not dissimilar question to the one I was asking myself,' she said. 'It's all about measuring…'

'…the probably unmeasurable. Would you like to continue the conversation over dinner on Saturday?'

He took her to the Cliff in Felixstowe, which he pronounced 'tolerable', and thought they should go to London
for their next night out. He kissed her for the first time on
Felixstowe beach, in the shadow of the pier.

If she was honest with herself, it was a moment she
had anticipated with anxiety; if she was not, she told herself
it would never happen anyway. The skin graft extended
only to just below his mangled ear so his lips were his own
but still, kissing would mean touching it. What would it feel
like? She thought of the unbridgeable gulf between the cel-
luloid surface of Adrian's photos and the skin welded to
the bones of their subjects, then that thought led to another. What if Philip was it? The bridge? What if Philip's rav-
aged face was the final line of the equation?

When he did kiss her, though, it felt nothing like solv-
ing an equation. She enjoyed the taste of beer on his
tongue, and fretted about losing her footing on the raked
shingle, and was exasperated by weather on the cusp of
spring which left her hands frozen and her cheeks aflame.
She worried her lipstick would smudge yet found the
smooth, cool hairlessness of his grafted skin marvellously
attractive, and then wondered if she was some kind of
freak. An even worse kind than a girl who enjoyed mathematics. Even as her body was pressed up against his, even
as she yielded him her mouth, and her nipples tingled and
everything between her knees and her belly-button turned
to jelly, somewhere a voice just like hers was whispering in
her ear that this wasn't the answer to anything, just a new
set of questions.

A moon a nail paring short of full had trodden a path
over the sea; sitting on the sea wall later, huddled into
Philip's overcoat, she noticed a small dark spot interrupting
the water's glitter.

'Look.' She pointed towards it. 'A seal moonbathing.'

But Philip could see nothing in the direction she was pointing. A little romance went out of the evening.

They married in the autumn of 1961. Both were certain about one another and neither wanted an elaborate ceremony. No point in waiting, they felt, in a world teetering on the brink of annihilation, on this farm being eaten away by wind and sea. No question, either, of anything but the Van Heppel family chapel, a tiny church with a thatched roof and a flint round tower, hidden behind the house in a grove of Scots pine. When Philip first showed it to her, making a rather silly pantomime of turning the great iron key in the lock, Ginny was disappointed, not for herself but for her parents, who worshipped at a somewhat grandiose Victorian neo-gothic establishment with a painted ceiling and a lot of brass. The Van Heppels' Holy Trinity had whitewashed walls studded with worn and mellowed plaques commemorating Philip's ancestors. Its lead-paned windows were of plain glass, only inconsistencies in the glazing giving some of them a pale green or amber hue. The sun, where its rays found their way between the trunks of the pines, cast honey-coloured lozenges across the stone-flagged floor and the higgledy rows of rush-backed chairs that served instead of pews. Even the altar cross, though solid silver, was bare of ornament. Once she had straightened the chairs, Ginny pronounced it perfect.

She was grateful to Maurice and Ronnie for offering to host the wedding, but she knew the force of obligation went more truly in the other direction. It was clear from their disproportionate excitement over the engagement that they had rated Philip's chances of marriage pretty low after his injury and had been adjusting themselves to the prospect that he would be the last of their line to live in the manor house and manage the land. Ronnie had embraced her a fraction too long when she, Frank and Alicia ('your

seconds,' Philip called them) had arrived for the engagement dinner, and had made a great play of explaining to
Ginny's awestruck mother that of course, darling Ginny
would have the family engagement ring and that their
'marvellous little man' in Hatton Garden was this very moment altering it to fit.

'Lovely emerald, been in the family for a century at
least. It'll bring out the colour of her eyes perfectly.'

Alicia thought Ginny should also wear Aunt Ronnie's
wedding dress.

'I could alter it for you easily, darling, you know I
could.' Ginny was certain Ronnie's wedding dress would be
far more beautiful than anything she could buy off the peg
in Manchester, but the choice of a wedding dress was a
debt she owed her mother, so she declined. What did it
matter anyway, what she wore?

Fittings required several trips home, where she found
her old room unchanged, her Spirograph in its box on her
childhood desk, the shelves above it where the Reader's
Digest Lives of the Great Scientists remained precisely
aligned, the street light's yellow sodium glow falling
through the thin curtains onto the satiny surface of the
pink nylon quilt. The evening before her final fitting, her
mother came in and sat beside her on the bed.

'Are you sure, dear?'

'I'm sure, mum. We're well-suited, Philip and I. We
can make a go of it.'

Her mother hesitated, twiddling her own wedding ring
around her finger. 'It's just...' She stared at Ginny's square-
cut emerald with a hunted expression, as if whatever she
was trying to say was going to have to be whipped out of
her. 'You're not marrying him for money, are you?' The
question came out in a rush, and, in the silence that followed, her mother's face seemed to collapse in on itself.

'Of course I'm not!' The notion was absurd; apart

from anything else, she had the impression the Van Heppels did not actually have much money. Although Philip was the farm manager, he worked alongside his hands, driving tractors, dipping sheep, castrating bullocks. The house, in the light of day, was genteelly shabby, as were Maurice and Ronnie and their grey Humber which had moss growing in the corners of its windows.

'His face, though…' Tears gathered in her mother's eyes.

'I'm used to it. I'll get more used to it.' Should she try to explain? Her mother would never understand. She didn't understand herself; it was irrational. The truth of it was, Philip's face had become a sort of talisman. As long as she could lay her fingers or her lips against that smooth, stretched skin, she was inoculated against the cataclysm that had stalked them all since the Russians built their wall across Berlin that summer. Philip represented the possibility of survival, the frail light shining in the gather of darkness.

She woke abruptly the next morning to the phone ringing in the front hall. She heard her mother answer, say, 'Just a moment, please,' and then her tread on the stairs.

'Ginny,' she said, poking her head around the door, 'there's someone on the phone for you. An American.' Her mother had been cultivating a studied nonchalance about Americans ever since meeting Frank, but it was still a work in progress. 'He says it's to do with your work.' An anxious gleam in her mother's eyes. Ginny's heart lurched, as the future she had conjured into being the previous evening when she tried to explain her feelings for Philip to her mother, seemed suddenly to disappear into the maw of the atomic sun.

She put on her dressing gown and followed her mother down the stairs. She sat on the cushioned telephone table seat, picked up the receiver and said,

'Hello?'

'Miss Matlock, Larry McGuire here. I hope you recall me from the Christmas Ball.'

She did but that had been more than half a year ago now and she had heard no more from him; if she thought of him at all, she supposed the Berlin Wall would have given him more than enough to do without pursuing her.

'How are you, Mr. McGuire?' She did her best to sound civil but, truth to tell, she was irritated, even angry, that he should have tracked her down to intrude on her happiness.

'I am extremely well, thank you, and I would like to congratulate you on your forthcoming marriage. Not long now, I understand.' She was tempted to ask him how he knew the date of her wedding, but that would be disingenuous.

'As you can imagine, Mr. McGuire, I have a lot to do, and I don't expect you called just to wish me well for my wedding.'

'That is true. You will be leaving us soon, and leaving Briar Cottage. So it seemed to me the time had come for us to have another chat. I am in Manchester now, as it happens. I could meet you at the buffet bar in Piccadilly Station.' Ginny blanked for a few seconds; Mancunians like her had not yet got used to the change of name and still thought of it as London Road.

'I really am very busy, Mr. McGuire, and I can't honestly think what we have to talk about that can't be discussed over the phone.'

'Indulge me, Miss Matlock. I can send a cab for you, and another to take you wherever you need to go after our meeting. I have no wish to intrude on your plans.'

'Well, you are doing. I have my final dress fitting at eleven, but if it will make you go away, I will agree to meet you. If you can arrange to have a cab here in, say, twenty minutes, I'll be able to spare you half an hour.'

Hiding behind the Official Secrets Act to make a vague excuse to her mother, she dressed and went outside to wait for her taxi, her mother's 'It'll be so nice once you're married and don't have to work anymore,' following her down the garden path. She hadn't intended to have breakfast before the dress fitting, so hardly noticed that she was too nervous to eat anyway.

McGuire was sitting at a corner table, an unremarkable man in a dark suit and a sober tie, a raincoat folded over his chair back. A trilby hat and two cups of coffee stood on the table, a stainless steel milk jug and sugar bowl between them. McGuire half-rose as she pulled out her chair; his eyes flickered over the Van Heppel emerald as she removed her gloves.

'Well, Mr. McGuire?' she asked, and took a sip of black coffee. Not even milk and certainly no sugar before the dress fitting. McGuire's cup remained untouched.

'British coffee,' he said with a sigh. 'However long I'm in this country, I don't think I'll ever get a taste for it.'

'Mr. McGuire, I'm not here to talk about coffee, though I will admit the stuff they serve in station buffets is particularly foul.' She favoured him with a brief smile.

'Understood.' He leaned towards her, resting his forearms on the table. 'Miss Matlock, what do you know about an organisation called the United World Federalists?'

'I've never heard of it.'

'You've never heard Frank Tettridge speak of it?'

'No, why? Tell me, Mr. McGuire, are you putting Alicia through this grilling too?'

'I can't comment on that, Miss Matlock.'

'You are.'

'If we could get back to my question, you've never

heard Frank mention the UWF? You've never seen correspondence relating to them?'

'I'm not in the habit of reading my housemates' letters.'

'Of course not, but sometimes things get left around and our eyes are drawn to them…'

'No. I've honestly never heard of this UWF. Who are they? What do they do?'

'The organisation was founded by a guy called Norman Cousins, a newspaper editor. He got the idea after visiting Hiroshima in 1949. Its members believe in world government. They think that's the best way of ensuring world peace.' McGuire's lab rat face looked sceptical. 'Frank Tettridge is a member of this organisation.'

'What's wrong with that? Surely world peace is a noble ambition, if perhaps an overly-optimistic one.'

'UWF is not what it seems. It's been infiltrated by communists, or perhaps it always was communist. Communist, federalist, you couldn't get a cigarette paper between them.'

'Correct me if I'm wrong, Mr. McGuire, but isn't the United States a federation?' McGuire blushed, he positively blushed! Ginny felt a surge of mischievous triumph; if she achieved nothing else in this life she would at least be able to tell her children she had once made a CIA agent blush.

'Your line makes me wonder, Miss Matlock, if there is more you could tell me about Frank but you don't wish to do so. For whatever reason…I find this disappointing.'

'I have told you the truth, Mr. McGuire. I had never heard of this UWF until now and I really don't think Frank is a communist.' The clothes, the records, the parcels from America. Then again, the phone number which Ginny had thought was Sue's, Frank's sudden trip to London after Ginny had called it, her breezy dismissal of her mother's alleged illness. Frank in such earnest conversation with the Artist whose existence she denied. Perhaps she was involved in something she shouldn't be. Perhaps Ginny should mention these things...

But it was already after ten o'clock and she couldn't be late for her dress fitting, and surely whatever Frank might be up to was harmless, though was anything tinged with communism harmless, and could Ginny herself be branded a traitor for saying nothing? What might Alicia have said? What if she were arrested? Even if she had done nothing wrong by failing to co-operate with McGuire, she could not marry Philip if she felt herself to be unpatriotic. Not after everything he had given for his country. She owed it to him, to this kind, funny, uncomplaining man she loved, to tell McGuire what she knew.

McGuire hailed her a cab outside the station, and she was only a couple of minutes late for the fitting. The dress was a perfect fit, and her mother cried quietly when she saw her in it, the tears sliding down her powdered cheeks even as she smiled and told Ginny how lovely she looked. The dressmaker brought out a slightly dusty decanter and a celebratory sherry was drunk. Ginny's mother wondered if they shouldn't go out to lunch, to Kendal's as it was a special occasion. Ginny hadn't the heart to refuse, though she felt irritable and out of sorts and moodily pushed a ham salad around her plate while her mother looked out for Coronation Street stars.

*

The night before her wedding, her last night at Briar Cottage, she dreamt. A blue-coloured dream, full of sighs and whisperings. She felt their breath on her ears, yet knew they were the voice of the sea. A sea discontented and restless. Out of the depths loomed a girl's face, a shifting halo of fair hair turned almost to frost by the blue filter of the water. The girl smiled. She smiled and smiled until she wore the grimace of the merman on the pub sign, until her mouth stretched to reveal rows of pearls, screwed into bloody gums. Phin's concrete pagodas shimmered into view, made insubstantial by the refracted light, occluded, then, by the appearance of a shadow. A head of long curls, a broad-shouldered figure tapering to a narrow waist and a fish's tail armoured with a glitter of scales, aqua, emerald, a pale primrose yellow. The figure raised its arm and an object floated free of its fingers, tiny and insubstantial next to the broad, splayed hand. She recognised the object but could not quite remember what it was…

Her eyes snapped open. In the crepuscular light falling through her curtains she could easily see Sue's pearl pendant hanging on the corner of her dressing table mirror. She looked at her alarm clock, whose fluorescent hands showed a quarter to six. In eight and a half hours, in little more than an ordinary working day, she would become Mrs. Philip Van Heppel.

The dream stayed with her, a cobweb caught on a corner of her mind as Alicia helped her dress, and Frank opened a bottle of Bollinger (did communists drink Bollinger, Ginny wondered?), and the toast she couldn't eat curled up on its plate, and beribboned cars came and went according to the traditional choreography until she and her father were left alone, silently gulping champagne because there was altogether too much to say and not enough time.

Ginny wore the dream as her something blue. She told herself it was right to have a dream to carry down the aisle because dreams are a tidying up of the brain, a sweeping of floors, a stacking of files. The dream was there to remind her that this part of her life was coming to a close and a new part was beginning.

# 10

By Christmas, Ginny was pregnant. She realised when she was sick in the field known as Right Angle Field, although it was plain to Ginny's eye that the field's angle was closer to 110 degrees. She had told Philip this, and they were walking the field so she could prove to him that, if the ploughman adjusted for the angle, he could dig at least five more furrows for sowing the summer wheat. She hadn't felt sick; the sight of her vomit among the clumps of soil and dead weeds came as a surprise to her as much as to Philip. Then it dawned on her; for a woman who counted everything, who had even counted her steps down the aisle and the pulse in her throat beating beneath Sue's pearl, she had been oddly negligent about counting the weeks since her last period. A good many of them, she realised now, feeling as if all the blood in her body had suddenly drained into her feet.

The baby would be born in July. A lovely summer baby! exclaimed the grandmothers to be. So good for birthday parties, said Ronnie. Better than having to lumber all through summer with the raging furnace of a growing child inside you, said Ginny's mother, Ginny having been born in November. You'll ripen with the wheat in the not-quite-Right Angle Field, said Philip, still wearing the silly grin that had been on his face now for several days and which really needed taking off and laundering. Cancer, said Frank. The birth sign, added Alicia, giving Frank a look. The three girls had done their best to keep up a connection, but without the common thread of working on the Island and their shared life at Briar Cottage, it was difficult, seemed sometimes to take more effort than it was worth. Pregnancy, Ginny quickly realised, carried her another step further from them and from her old life.

Although Ginny ripened, the wheat did not. Spring came early, but then gave way to frosts in April. It rained through June. The Americans had more than a hundred nuclear missiles in Izmir now, on the Black Sea, all pointed at Moscow. There was a night during calving when the vet had to be called out to twins. Ginny came downstairs in her dressing gown intending to make coffee while Philip and the vet were out in the calving shed, but when they came back in, they found her sitting at the kitchen table in some sort of reverie. She had no idea how long she had been sitting there, but her back was very stiff and she had pins and needles in her feet. Collecting herself, she pointed the vet to the downstairs cloakroom where he could wash up, put on the kettle and opened a packet of custard creams. Her hand had gone first to the bourbons, but she knew she would eat them all herself once the packet was opened so she chose the custard creams instead. The baby didn't like custard creams nearly as much.

'What happened to you?' asked Philip, once the vet had left and they had gone back up to bed. He wore a concerned expression but his voice betrayed his exasperation; they had lost one of the calves and the vet thought it unlikely they would be able to breed from the cow again.

'I don't really know. I could hear her, the cow. I knew what was happening to her, what it meant to her.'

'Darling, don't be so ridiculous. The calving barn is nowhere near in hearing distance, and the cow is just a cow. Nothing means anything to a cow except feed. It must have been the wind. You know how these easterlies sound in the chimney. Pregnancy does funny things to women's imaginations. I read about it somewhere.' He turned away from her, pulling the bedclothes up to his mangled ear and reaching to extinguish the bedside light. She lay awake long after he had begun to gently snore, exploring this set of emotions called imagination, an attribute she had never seen the need of nor believed she possessed. What was it her college tutor had written on the board at the beginning of his first lecture? About the doctrine of right and wrong being contestable but that of lines and figures not so? She couldn't remember who had said it or exactly what they had said, but she had never lost sight of its meaning. Until now, it seemed.

She became increasingly distracted. Some Sundays, after church, she and Philip would go back with Frank and Alicia for a sherry at the cottage. She knew Philip would have preferred The Merman, where he could enjoy a pint of beer, but she could not bring herself to go in there. She was surprised that Frank, of all people, seemed to understand her feelings and supported her vigorously when she said she would prefer a drink at the cottage. She could easily bring a jug of beer from the pub for Philip, and the chairs in the cottage were more comfortable, though Ginny was increasingly unable to heave herself out of any of them but the hard, upright dining chairs.

The conversation – gossip from the Island, gossip about family and mutual friends in London – seemed to swirl around Ginny without ever touching her. Only if asked a direct question could she manage to focus long enough to answer it and then she slipped away again, to the place in this newly discovered imagination where the castle stood darkling on its mound and the Artist plied his brushes. Sometimes she thought vaguely about her conversations with Larry McGuire and wondered how it was that Frank was still there, if her solicitude was evidence of changed ways, or perhaps some double-blind because she knew all about those conversations and had kept a step ahead of them? But she could no longer work her way through the logic of such a proposition so abandoned it. Eventually she began to find it too complicated to go out at all and excused herself even from church. God approved of pregnancy, didn't He? She felt sure He would understand.

Philip's former nanny was brought back and took up residence in the small room next to the nursery as if she had never been away. Mr. and Mrs. Van Heppel had been living in this very house, she told Ginny, when Master Philip was born and old Mr. Van Heppel was still rattling about the Manor. Nanny wore a grey dress with a pie crust collar, immaculately pressed but shiny with wear about the seams and a little too tight across the bust. By the look of it, she had worn the same dress when Master Philip was a baby, and, in Ginny's mind, it quickly came to stand for everything Nanny had to say about childcare. She had clearly not seen fit to acquaint herself with Dr. Spock. Nor had Ginny, if she was honest, but Alicia had given her a copy of Baby and Childcare and she had dipped into it once or twice. It made her very tired.

She had persuaded herself that looking after the baby would be no more than an extension of pregnancy, that her body would know what to do, leaving her mind free to return to its work. But, despite Nanny's dictates and Dr. Spock's recommendations, pints of Guinness from Ronnie and a bottle steriliser supplied by her mother, the baby would not feed. He turned his face from Ginny's cracked nipples, the skin of her breasts as taut and burning as Philip's skin grafts with mastitis and humiliation. Philip tried to console her by saying he found her engorged breasts irresistible even if the baby didn't, but she was too tired and battered for love-making. Nanny could get up to the baby in the night, said Philip, and Nanny said he would sleep better anyway if he was given a bottle at bedtime. But his every cry tore through the frayed fabric of her sleep, sending her stumbling to the nursery, udders swaying beneath her damp-fronted nightdress. Everything was anarchy and chaos and she was nothing but a milch cow without the brain to make any sense of it.

She had to get back to work.

She took to sitting at the desk in the farm office, the account books open in front of her, but the columns of figures might as well have been Egyptian hieroglyphs for all the sense she could make of them. Even though she knew the baby was safe with Nanny, or Ronnie, she was still convinced she could hear him crying.

She had to get away from the farm.

She took to walking on the headland which marked the seaward boundary of the Van Heppel estate, where it sheared away to the beach and the channel of gunmetal water she used to cross every morning to the Island. The shape of the Island was changing. More radio masts bristled from its back and Phin, she could see, had been busy constructing more of his experiments in concrete. New sets of calculations, new deductions, fresh minds, moving on without her. A new urgency; there were rumours in the papers that the

Russians were preparing to put missiles on Cuba, which was only ninety miles from the east coast of America. New York schools had begun duck and cover drills and they were re-opening the air raid shelters in Central Park.

She fancied the southern tip of the Island had blunted, eroded by the cross-currents, but she knew that couldn't be the case, not in the matter of months since Bonn had brought it to her attention. Yet it wasn't months, was it? This was 1962, almost two years since she had first come to Aldeford. They had an IBM machine in Section Four now, Frank had told her, which could do all the calculations Ginny used to do in a fraction of the time.

She turned away, looked south, past the Island to the open sea, breathed the astringent air deep into her lungs and let them expel the cloying stink of nappy buckets and vomity matinée jackets. The cranes of Felixstowe stalked the horizon, alien as Wells' Martians. A late summer gale was blowing itself out, herding plump grey clouds before it, making a Jew's harp of the marram grass. A spit of rain stung her cheeks. She turned her back to the wind and gazed across a patchwork of Van Heppel fields to where the tall barley twist chimneys of the manor house were just visible in a dip between acres of wheat stubble and the Anguses gathered under the great oak which dominated their summer pasture. They too had their black, bony rumps to the wind. She felt utterly alone, stranded in some no-man's land between the two worlds she loved and which had given her identity. If only she could wind back time to before the baby, when it was just her and Philip and their plans, or fast forward it until the baby could walk and feed itself and went to school all day. If only she could return to the Island. The IBM machine needed someone to feed it the right information in order to make its calculations correctly. That, she could do.

Looking back out to sea she noticed a solitary figure on the beach and recognised it, from the pale hair whipping in the wind, as the Artist. She should start homeward, she had been out a long time, but she had not seen the Artist since that Christmas ball nearly two years ago at which she had met Philip and she was curious. His appearance, just as she was considering the possibility of returning to the Island, seemed like a good omen. She started for the beach, along the dun-coloured strand, until she was close enough to the Artist to look over his shoulder and see what he was working on. He showed no evidence of having noticed her but she knew he must have done, knew his senses to be uncannily acute. Like an animal's, she had thought sometimes, in the past.

In the painting, fire predominated, exquisitely rendered in golds and oranges, maple reds and molten whites. She could feel the heat of it on her skin and took a step back.

'What is that?'

'I don't know,' he replied. He showed no surprise at her presence, and she was gripped by a certainty that he had known all along she would walk this way and had been waiting for her. He did not even turn to look at her or lift his brush from the canvas. 'Perhaps something I remember?' he added, re-loading his brush with paint. 'Perhaps something to come.'

'You'd think the pain of such a thing would be inexpressible and yet, here it is. You have done it.'

'I paint because I have no words.'

She looked again at the canvas and saw that he had conjured a face from the fire, the flames framing it like red hair. 'For what? For this? Did this happen to you? Is that why you walk with a stick?'

'I'm like your husband,' he said. 'I have been damaged by both fire and water.'

'You were a pilot too?'

'Not of war planes.'

'You should tell her. I think the time has come.' Surely the voice was Frank's! Ginny whipped around from the painting to see Frank behind her, appeared as if from nowhere. She shifted her gaze from the painting to Ginny, but a residue of its fiery light seemed to linger around her, so her red hair, even the pale skin of her face, glowed against the dark clouds. Ginny felt frightened; it was irrational, she knew, but her grasp on reason had become tenuous since the arrival of the baby.

'Are you...are you both part of this...United Federalists, or whatever it's called?' she blurted out, suddenly appalled by guilt. Her voice sounded whiny. 'To be honest, I can't see what's wrong with it. McGuire said it had been infiltrated by the Russians but...'

'Oh shut up, Ginny. This gentleman and I go way further back than the United World Federalists, though McGuire is right about that, I am a member and I do use my work here to help them out from time to time. If only some countries have nuclear weapons, there can never be equality. Either everyone has them or no-one does. Only then can you begin to dismantle the nation state and bring an end to war. I don't much care which way it goes, as long as it leads to complete freedom of movement and the equal sharing of resources.'

'So you are a spy.'

'If you say so. I'd call myself a freedom fighter.'

'Why are you still here? Surely you can't...do anything useful if the CIA is on to you?'

'Nor can I leave. I have to protect you, whether I like it or not.'

'Protect me? What on earth are you talking about?'

'She doesn't know what she's talking about.' The Artist

113

spoke softly, but his voice seemed to command the weather so his words fell into a sudden silence with the clarity of stones dropping into a still pond. He had risen from his camping stool; he looked taller than Ginny remembered. 'She's a fantasist. Surely that's obvious from her political beliefs.' He gave his harsh laugh, that sound like the barking of a seal. Frank made no reply, and when Ginny looked for her, she could no longer see her. She seemed to have vanished as abruptly as she had come.

Yet the painting, the painting seemed to have come to life. It pulsed and undulated, the firelight in it flaring and dying as if the fire were actual and not a contrivance of brush and pigment. She could see, now, that the profile in the flames was one of those tromp l'oeil effects whereby a single outline showed two figures facing one another. One profile was clearly that of the Artist himself but the other... the other was surely Frank, the flames arranged around her head unmistakably in the style of her hair.

'Boats, ships,' the Artist remarked, resuming their earlier conversation as if Frank had never been there. 'I used to pilot vessels navigating the shallows along this stretch of coast. I knew the seabed, where the deep channels were, and the sandbars. I knew the currents. Now, well... Terrible things can happen when you're taken away from what you know, from your element, as it were.'

Frank was wrong, thought Ginny. You had to care. You couldn't uninvent the Bomb but you could make it secure. You couldn't make the world a safer place by releasing such a technology to everyone but by concentrating it to such a terrifying extent it became unusable. She looked out towards the Island, only half a mile away, yet its outline blurred as a sheet of rain blew across it.

'I understand,' said Ginny, taking a step towards the water, towards the Island. Her mind was clear now. If she could only get there she could return to Section Four, to her own element. She could prevent terrible things from happening.

'If you want to swim for it, go. All will be well. The sea knows all our fears and dreams and is not to be denied.' She had heard something like this before, she was certain, but could not remember where or when. A long time ago, she thought.

Another step, and the incoming tide was lapping at her boots. The sea showed itself as orderly, its gathering waves lined up like furrows, neatly contained between the horizon and the shore. She plotted a straight line between herself and the Island, saw her body following it, powerful and un-hesitating, the water closing neatly in her wake. Unlacing her boots, she tossed them up the beach behind her, did the same with her clothes until she was stripped down to her underwear.

'I'll swim with you,' said the Artist, rising to his un-steady feet and unwinding the scarf from his neck. 'I'll be your pilot.' He stripped off his long coat and something gleamed silver in the tail of her eye. She heard a splash as he followed her into the water, and felt herself borne up and out towards the horizon as if on the back of a great fish. The hand of the universe was guiding her to the Is-land, to the space shaped for her to occupy and the work she was intended to do in it. She no longer had to think, merely press her finger lightly to the trigger in her brain which set all the right bits of it in motion.

# 11

For a long time, even after she had been discharged from the clinic, Ginny continued in a kind of half life, vaguely aware of light and dark circling one another through a gap in the curtains and faces revolving like planets around her dimmed room. Voices reached her as an indistinct hum, as if heard from the other side of a wall. She was cocooned in cloud, occasionally pierced by a spoonful of soup or a needle in her arm. The soup seemed meaningless, but she came to yearn for the needles, for the sharp, clean puncture to the skin and the spread of warmth and indolence which followed it, as if some distilled essence of summer holiday was flowing through her veins instead of blood. The feeling didn't last long, though, and between times it was more like the wet days of holidays, whose emptiness filled up with boredom and irritation. Sometimes Ginny thought she would be able to get out of bed if only it weren't for the weight of the boredom.

When Philip's face orbited into view, and she read the worry in his eyes, etched on to the living half of his face, she tried to tell him there was nothing to worry about, there never had been, she had always been safe with the Artist. But what made perfect sense in her mind seemed to become jumbled when she tried to put it into words. Whenever she tried to bring the Artist into focus, her memory was disrupted by a sort of radio static, some images broken and distorted, some lost altogether. What had happened to him? Why had no-one mentioned him when it must have been he, after all, who saved her? Why had he not been to visit her? Were they keeping him away from her? Had he drowned, and they were shying away from telling her until she was stronger? She wanted to think he had carried on swimming, describing his perfect arc through the water, because then she could smile at Philip and see her smile mirrored by his. She hated making Philip unhappy but remained apparently incapable of doing otherwise.

A recollection emerged from the fog of her brain. When Philip came to visit her in the hospital after the baby was born, he had gazed down into the crib and said how marvellous it was to think that his son would have no memory of his father without his scars, how, in the baby's eyes, his face would become normal. She hadn't known. Every few months Philip would go up to London to see his specialist. He had to be careful of exposing the grafted skin to the sun, applying a prescribed ointment and cramming his MCC sunhat on to his head whenever he was working outdoors in the summer. Every time he'd crack the same bad joke about Virgil having got it wrong and farming being the last job for a wounded soldier, but they had never had a serious conversation about his disfigurement. She could see, now, that this was all her fault. She had believed the fact of her was enough for him, had seen only the skin and not the scars. And now even the fact of her made him unhappy. She had failed as a wife and mother, and now even as a patriot.

Frank had not been to visit her either. When she asked about this, she was told only close family was permitted, but she knew this was another lie; she could tell from their faces, their tones of voice. They sounded like adults assuring a child Father Christmas was real, even though the simplest calculation made it clear he could not be. When she tried to protest, they gave her another injection. But the time between the injections gradually stretched out, and Ginny came to accept that only blood ran in her veins, not summer sun, or boredom, or protest, or anything else that was not to be found in the veins of a rational woman. On some days, to begin with, she found it difficult to trust the evidence of her own eyes when she examined the blue delta of blood vessels in her wrists, and felt compelled, as any scientist would, to test this hypothesis by observation. Having no knife or scissors to hand, she broke an empty tea cup she found on the bedside table and used a pottery shard to open a small vein. The nurse who administered the injections reappeared after that, smelling of fresh air and oiled bicycle chain, and Ginny's drinks were delivered thereafter in the tin mugs from the picnic basket. The precautions were ridiculous. She had satisfied herself empirically that there was indeed nothing but blood in her veins, and she hadn't been so stupid as to cut the artery.

Eventually the nurse cycled away for the last time, Ginny watching her progress down the drive from a chair set in the bay of the bedroom window. The following day, she dressed and went downstairs, clinging to the banister, the Artist's strange, weak legs suddenly in her mind. She was not in her own home but in the manor house.

'Just so we can keep an eye on you,' said Ronnie, with

a strained smile. 'Spoil you a bit.' She reached out a hand to Ginny's arm. Beneath her blouse and cardigan, and her needle-scored skin, was little more than bone and nerves, and she felt the full weight and shape of her mother-in-law's touch. 'I'm so sorry, dear,' the smile crumpled, 'we had no idea. Everyone thinks, you know, when you have a baby, it's a happy time…'

'What happened to the Artist?' She didn't want to hear about the baby; she had almost managed to forget its existence.

'Who?'

'The Artist,' insisted Ginny, shaking with the effort. 'He was with me on the beach. He came into the water with me and then…I don't know what happened to him. If you're keeping something from me, please don't. I need to know. He…he's important to me. Frank was there too. I've been wanting to ask her but you wouldn't let me see her.'

'Just as well, by the sounds of it,' said Ronnie. 'Come on, come into the kitchen. Let me get you something to eat. You'll feel better with a square meal inside you.' A square meal was Ronnie's remedy for every ill. For Ginny, it had always been a conundrum, because only sandwiches were square and they were not meals. Nevertheless, she allowed herself to be led along the whitewashed passage to the domestic offices at the rear of the house. She sat obediently at the big farmhouse kitchen table and waited, picking at a knot in the pine while Ronnie fussed about at the Aga. There were occasions, she knew, when the solutions to conundrums must be allowed to present themselves in their own good time. Ronnie put down a mug of tea and a plate of scrambled eggs on toast in front of her and sat across the corner of the table from her, pondering briefly as she stirred sugar into her tea before looking up and saying,

'There was no-one with you, dear. No-one at all. Philip

thought you'd been gone too long and went looking for you. The weather had got up and he didn't think you ought to be out in it. He called the coastguard.'

'No, that's not right. I'd gone on to the beach to talk to the Artist. He must have…I don't know…Surely someone must have found his painting things and wondered… And Frank was there. She was.'

'No, Ginny. There was nothing on the beach other than your clothes. Not this artist, whoever he is, not Frank. Frank's…well, never mind that now.' Ronnie reached out her hand, placed it over Ginny's where it lay beside the untouched plate. 'You're still not at all well, are you, dear? Eat now.' Understanding this was a test of her restoration, Ginny forced herself to take a bite. She needed to go home, to escape her mother-in-law's vigilance. She needed to return to the beach to see for herself. She needed to find that picture and work out its meaning. She needed to talk to Frank. Once she had managed to swallow the masticated lump of toast and eggs she said,

'I'm fine, honestly. I should go home. I can't imagine how Philip is coping with…with the baby.'

'I don't think you're ready yet. Let us take care of you a bit longer. Philip has Nanny.'

The days passed in a kind of languor, as though time moved more slowly inside the manor house than it did beyond its walls. Ginny prowled the corridors, her resolve weakened, her scattered brain gathering itself towards what came most naturally to it and freed her from having to think. She counted her steps and calculated the passing of time by the angles of shadows and the parallelograms of light falling through windows. 360 degrees divided by twenty-four hours equals fifteen degrees per hour. She counted apples in bowls and the volume of sherry in the decanter on the sideboard. She measured the stumbling pulse in her throat, where her fingers sought, out of habit, Sue's pearl. She kept forgetting it had been lost during the rescue. Sometimes she paused beside the telephone in the hall, intending to call Briar Cottage, but there was always someone in earshot, it seemed. A member of the household staff, or Ronnie, hovering solicitously.

On occasion, as long as Philip was there too, Nanny would bring the baby over from the old steward's house and set him in Ginny's lap. The first time this happened, she froze. It was possible, she thought, that she had died in her chair and rigor mortis had set in, but no, she could feel the solid weight of the child's terry-padded bottom on her thighs, and it made her nauseous. She didn't think the dead could feel nauseous. Gradually, however, her body learned to respond to the baby's presence, to prop his furzy little head against her arm and inhale his scent of milk and Johnson's Baby Powder. Once, left alone with him for a few moments, she found herself speaking to him. All in a rush she told him how sorry she was not to be a proper mother to him but you see, what she lived for, what gave her a purpose in the world, was mathematics. Perhaps, when he was older, he would find a calling too and would understand, although she didn't know, it struck her not many people felt as she did, about anything. Then Philip came back into the room and she fell silent, and let him respond to the baby's gurgles.

'Do you think,' he asked her, once Nanny had carried the baby off again, 'you might feel well enough to start thinking about a christening? Mother's worrying he won't fit the family gown if we leave it too much longer. He's getting really quite bonny.'

Without me, she thought.

\*

121

A warm Saturday afternoon at the end of September, one of those wistful days when the sun pours molten gold over the landscape yet the shadows are long and dusk falls early. Ginny was in the library. Outside, she could hear Ronnie in the garden, the snip of secateurs, words exchanged with the gardener and with Nanny, who had taken the baby out to air in his pram. Muffled by the glass, sounds dropped into the deep silence of the library like pebbles into a pool.

Reading anything other than newspaper headlines remained beyond her, and she avoided those because the rising tension between America and Russia merely deepened her desperation to be back on the Island. She gravitated to the library because nobody else used it. No fire had been lit there for many years, and Ginny hankered to draw the still, cold air deep into her lungs. It made her feel clean, the way walks beside the sea did, but she was not supposed to take those any more, not alone at least. Well to hell with that! It was a beautiful day, perhaps one of the last of the year, and, if she slipped out of the scullery door while Ronnie was in the garden, her absence wouldn't be noticed. The household staff had Saturday afternoons off unless the family was entertaining. She didn't even need to collect a coat on an afternoon such as this.

It was not until she saw the telephone box in Little Alde, a hamlet which straggled along the road half way between Aldeford and the Manor, that her intention became clear to her. She had told herself she would walk this way to avoid being spotted on Van Heppel land, but that wasn't it at all. She entered the booth and, having brought no money with her, made a reverse charge call to Briar Cottage, hoping against hope that Frank and Alicia had not gone out for the afternoon. The phone seemed to ring for a long time, but eventually Alicia answered, sounding, Ginny thought, rather strained and cautious, as if she had been waiting for a call she didn't want.

'Hello, Alicia,' she said.

'Ginny! Darling!' The relief in Alicia's voice was palpable. 'So lovely to hear from you. How are you? And where are you? Why the reverse charges?'

'Oh, I was just out for a walk and decided to call on impulse. I didn't have my handbag with me.'

'OK.' She could tell from Alicia's tone how feeble her explanation sounded.

'Actually, I'd love to come and see you. I'm in the phone booth in Little Alde. Maybe Frank could come and fetch me in the jeep? I don't think I could manage the whole distance on foot yet.' That would give her a chance to talk to Frank without Alicia; she was unsure how much, if anything, Alicia really knew about Frank.

There was a pause. Ginny wondered if they had been cut off. 'Alicia? Are you still there?'

'Yes. Nobody told you about Frank, then?'

'What about Frank?' She felt suddenly cold and weak; the air in the phonebox was dank and urine-smelling.

'It was dreadful, Ginny. She was arrested. I think it must have been around the same time you…had your accident. That would explain why no-one told you, perhaps. She's been accused of,' Alicia's voice dropped almost to a whisper, 'spying for the Russians. And you know, with all the rumours flying around at the moment about what they might do…well, enough said about that on a public phone line…All these men came to the house in the middle of the night, one I'd seen before around the base,' McGuire, thought Ginny, 'and some others. They broke some of her records, and they were waving guns about for heaven's sake!'

'And during the close season,' said Ginny, marvelling

at herself. Both of them laughed, even though Ginny felt sick at the thought of herself spilling the beans to McGuire in the Piccadilly Station café. What had she set in motion?

'My,' said Alicia, 'you've been learning fast from Cousin Philip. We'll make a country lady of you yet.'

'I doubt Philip will let me handle a shotgun any time soon,' said Ginny ruefully, and realised, with a lifting of her heart which seemed perverse in the circumstances, that this was the first time she had been able to refer to her breakdown with anything approaching detachment. She had been right to tell McGuire what she did; it had been her patriotic duty and she could not blame herself for the consequences.

'Look, darling, let's not talk about this anymore on the phone. Come over. Start walking and I'll send a cab to meet you.'

Having walked a considerable distance towards Aldeford before the cab found her, Ginny was relieved to reach the cottage, but it was a forlorn place now without Frank's boisterous presence and her red Dansette. The angled space under the stairs was cobwebbed and marked by the ghosts of the player and its records where the paint had faded around them and left their ghosts. Alicia had lit a fire and made some scones, but the shadow of the castle seemed to reach through the window and smother the fire's brightness and the welcoming scent of fresh baking. Despite the fire, the room was noticeably colder than the balmy afternoon outside. Ginny wondered if she should suggest taking their chairs into the garden but didn't want Alicia to think her efforts were unappreciated. She contented herself with,

'It must be rather queer, being on your own here.'

'It's horrible. I'm not staying. I'm leaving at the end of next month, going back home for a while and then we'll see. A job in London, hopefully…if we're all still alive by then. I did think of marrying Bonn, but marriage, well it rather suggests you believe in a future. I probably shouldn't say this, but I suppose you're still covered by the Act?'

'For the rest of my born days, I think.'

'Word is, the Russians are definitely putting missiles on Cuba.'

'I can see the sense of that kind of balance. It would make sure neither of them actually fired one for fear of retaliation.'

'In your logical world, Ginny, but is Khruschev logical? Is Kennedy for that matter? Some of the guys in the liaison office say he takes so many painkillers for his back he doesn't know what day of the week it is half the time! And then there are the mistakes, the false alarms. Have you any idea how often those happen? And that's just the ones we get to hear about out here on the edge of civilisation.'

'I wish I was still on the Island.'

'Gosh, do you?' Alicia paused in the course of pouring tea, waving the pot in the air in a somewhat hectic manner. 'You're not unhappy with Philip, are you? I was so pleased when you married him. He's a lovely man, and you just seemed to get each other, if you know what I mean.'

'I'm not unhappy with Philip at all. Now please put that teapot down before you drop it.'

'Gosh, yes, sorry.'

'I just don't see why I can't be happy with Philip and have my job. It's important work and I'm good at it.'

'Well, they have that IBM thing in Section Four now. It's an absolute monster! They've had to put up a whole new building for it! And you've got a baby.'

'The "monster" has to have someone feed it numbers to process. I think I could manage that better than feeding the baby, to be honest.'

Alicia looked momentarily shocked but recovered herself quickly, plastering a warm smile over her distress. 'Has he got a name yet?'

Ginny shook her head. She took a bite out of her scone and complimented it even though it was rather dense. But her long walk had made her properly hungry for the first time in ages, and she found she had a nostalgia for Alicia's diabolical cooking. Neither of them mentioned the baby again.

She arrived back at the Manor just as dusk was falling and the postman, having made his evening delivery, was bumping down the potholed drive on his bicycle. A scene, thought Ginny, which had been played out on the Manor drive since bicycles and the GPO were invented.

'Airmail letter for you, Mrs. Philip,' he called as he passed, unable to keep such an excitement to himself.

The arrival of the airmail letter had caused Ginny to be missed. The household was in quite a flurry when she came in; she could hear the baby, no doubt affected by the general disturbance, screaming in the kitchen, from which direction Philip emerged, his good cheek flushed and his single brow drawn down in a worried frown.

'There you are!' he exclaimed, opening his arms to her. 'Thank God!' She went to him and leaned her head against his chest. His heart made a steady, hollow kind of thud, like heavy feet crossing an empty room.

'I went to see Alicia. I'm sorry, I should have said, but it was a spur of the moment thing.'

'I'd have thought you'd know better by now.' Ronnie, emerging from the drawing room with a sherry glass in her hand. 'You frightened us half to death! So irresponsible, selfish.'

'Alright, Ma, that's enough. She's back now, that's all that matters.' Ronnie harrumphed, but demurred. Ginny thought perhaps her curiosity about the airmail letter had trumped the urge to give her daughter-in-law a piece of her mind. She leaned closer into Philip and felt his arms tighten around her. She felt safe in their encircling, knowing Ronnie never took issue with the men. It wasn't done.

'I saw the postman on my way in. He said there was a letter for me?' Raising her head from Philip's chest she could see it, an oblong of light blue, alone on the scratched salver where the post was habitually left, as if cut loose from the sky above the clouds and fallen to earth of its own volition. She picked it up and was surprised to find it had any weight at all. The stamps were American. She did not recognise the handwriting in which it was addressed.

'I'm going up to change,' she announced, feeling all their eyes upon her as she mounted the stairs with the letter in her hand.

Inside the airmail wrapper she found a loose sheet of thin paper. This handwriting she did recognise. Frank's. She was not surprised – after all, who else did she know in America – but her hand shook as she began to read, setting up a soft rustling in the paper. The letter was dated several weeks earlier.

*Dear Ginny,*

*I'm uncertain if this letter will reach you but I write in the hope that it does. I will not be able to post it myself but will entrust to friends who have promised to do so for me. I won't go into my circumstances here, you'll learn them soon enough.*

A sudden vision of Frank in a striped prison suit, with her red hair shaved and her wrists and ankles shackled, distracted Ginny from her reading. She chided herself; that was what prisoners looked like in the movies, not in real life. She read on:

*I guess you must have worked out by now, with that big brain of yours, that your Artist is the figure known to me, and to legend, as the Merman. But you'll be wondering about my connection to him and why you saw me on the beach that day when – you were right – I should have left already and when I had denied his existence, just as I did to Sue, who saw him too. In the library at Aldeford Manor there is a little book entitled Myths and Legends of the Suffolk Coast. Look up the Aldeford Merman in there and you will find that the Warden of the castle at that time, the man responsible for the tortures so graphically depicted on the walls of the pub, was one Odon de la Tête Rouge. My father's family claim descent (and our hair) from him and the Merman has been exacting his revenge on us ever since. I will not trouble you here with the whole catalog of Tettridge family tragedies. I have very little time in which to write this and must stick to what is important.*

*I loved Sue Reynolds very much. UWF, which I had joined while I was at university, backed me to take the job on the Island, otherwise I would never in a month of Sundays have set foot on this spot! Then the gods sent me Sue and we were happy for a while, until she started to see the Merman. You know what happened next because it nearly happened to you too. Sue didn't die in an accident, nor did she drown herself. He lured her into the water, he murdered her, Ginny. He believed I would follow her but he reckoned without my sense of mission regarding the work I was there to do. World peace matters more to me than my personal happiness.*

*I disliked you on sight, Ginny, perhaps because you were not Sue, but I doubt we would ever have become friends anyway. We're just too different. That was a relief. I thought we would both be safe and the Merman would go back to sea for another generation. I underestimated him, of course. He has had centuries to refine his strategies and I have had nothing but twenty-five years of rational Americans assuring me the legend is nonsense. He used that sharp mind of yours against us both, to ensure I would get caught. You see, I do know you answered McGuire's questions but I don't hold it against you. You weren't acting independently but under the compulsion of the Tettridge curse.*

So Frank would absolve her from blame, yet by doing so would also deprive her of agency. Whether or not she ever saw the Artist again, Frank would haunt her to the end of her days.

*Which is why I'm writing this. Not for some salvation trip but because you've made your life in Aldeford now and you need to know what you're up against. Keep watch, Ginny, he's made good use of you once, he might try to do it again. Keep watch over your child especially.*

*Frank*

She did not know how long she might have sat there, on the side of her bed, staring out of the window over a patchwork of ploughland and pasture gradually receding into darkness. The first stars were up. The letter lay in her lap, lifting from time to time in the breeze coming through the open window, as if she needed reminding it was there.

A soft knock came on the door. Philip's voice, muffled, wary, calling her name, calling her back into her life. She tore the letter into a confetti of tiny pieces and tossed them out of the window where they caught the breeze and scattered. The letter was Frank's fantasy. Ginny didn't begrudge it, if it helped Frank to weather her imprisonment, but she had done the right thing, talking to McGuire. It had nothing to do with any so-called curse. McGuire had promised her anonymity and she had never mentioned the conversation to Philip. What good would it do for him to know about it now? What difference would it make to any of them if what Alicia feared came to pass? Would they let prisoners out, she wondered, if the Russians launched a nuclear attack?

'Everything alright?' asked Philip through the door.

'Yes, of course. I'm fine. You don't have to wait out there.' He came in. 'Funny man,' she said affectionately.

'I'm uncertain of you, Ginny, ' he said, sitting on the bed beside her.

'I'm sorry. There's no need to be. I'm alright now, honestly.' She took his hand. 'Let's go home tomorrow. We should make the best of things.'

'That's an odd way of putting it.'

It had been, he was right. A disfigured phrase, alarming evidence of how deeply she had internalised Alicia's sense of an ending. 'I mean the very best, the best life has to offer. No half measures.' She put her arms around his neck and drew him in for a kiss. He needed a haircut, she thought, as her fingers slid around the base of his skull. He smelled of turned earth and the grassy breath of cows.

At dinner that night, Ginny ate well, and found the more she ate, the better the food tasted. She was saddened by the unloved thinness of her arms. Keep watch over your child, Frank had written, but such thin arms could offer no protection to a child. By dessert, she had summoned the strength to raise the now pressing subject of the christening. Before the end of October, she thought, before Alicia left, before the weather finally turned and the baby's arms grew too fat for the family gown's little puffed sleeves.

'But darling, we haven't chosen a name yet,' said Philip, beaming with pleasure.

'Oh, Philip, I think, don't you? Philip Maurice Brian. Brian for my dad. Pip for short.'

'P.M.B. Van Heppel,' Maurice intoned. 'Look alright on the honours board at Lords, that will.'

The candlelight moved kindly over their hands and faces, over the women's rings and the lead crystal wine glasses and the oak-panelled walls. It warmed and animated Philip's grafted skin.

'To Pip.' Maurice raised his glass. 'May all his expectations be great.'

'To Pip,' they murmured, laughing gently at Maurice's literary joke.

The date was set for the 28th October, cutting it fine but that was the earliest date the bishop was available. Ronnie was insistent on the bishop. The gown was already a little snug , but Alicia worked wonders with some discreet lace gores cut from Ginny's wedding veil.

'At every key point in my life,' said Ginny, sipping a martini while Alicia sewed and Pip lay on the hearthrug, trying to turn over, 'there you are with your needle.'

'I'm your fairy godmother.'

'Are you sure? What if I pricked my finger on that needle? Might I fall asleep for a hundred years?'

'Ah, but I'm not your fairy godmother any more, am I? I'm Pip's.' Alicia beamed at the baby, who rewarded her with a solemn frown before flopping on to his front like a lolloping seal. Alicia applauded. 'And you won't be doing any sewing, will you, darling boy?'

Ginny drained her glass and popped the olive in her

mouth. 'Another?' she asked, holding up her empty glass and moving towards the drinks trolley.

'Why not? Almost done with the close work. Then we'll try it on him, shall we?'

The morning of the christening dawned overcast and still. The Sunday front pages were dominated by grainy photos of vessels, said to be Russian and said to be carrying cargoes of warheads, steaming towards Kennedy's quarantine zone around Cuba. Gazing out of the bedroom window as she dressed, Ginny watched rooks rising from the trees bordering the Right Angle Field to begin their day; a day which seemed little more than a thinning of night into a grey fret which coated everything in a slick of moisture and caught in the back of the throat with a vague smell of burning. The walk to the chapel, Pip bundled inside his father's Barbour to protect him from the damp, felt more like wading. The sea's bustle carried clearly across the Sunday silence.

She held Pip herself at the font as he cried when handed to Alicia and the bishop seemed discomfited by the din. Neither of his godfathers, her little brother Joe and a friend of Philip's from his schooldays, had the faintest idea how to handle a baby. He was slippery as a fish in her arms, but, once the bishop had finished with the oil and water and salt (you'd think we were going to put him on a barbecue, said Philip, for whom the Church of England was merely a state of being rather than a religion), he quietened. A small surge of pride went through her, that she had calmed him where Alicia could not, and a dim sense of something deeper and more visceral, that she, and only she, made him safe. She dipped her head to kiss the whorls of pale hair on his head.

He looked steadily back at her as if he knew exactly what she was thinking. His eyes, she noticed, were so light they seemed to take on the hue of everything around him, from the candlelit walls to the underwater gloaming outside the chapel windows. So strangely wise that looking into them seemed to lead her into a looking-glass world where all the power was his and she was the helpless one. Something began to dazzle and blur in the tail of her eye. She blinked to clear her vision. Then the bishop pronounced the Dismissal and the small congregation began to shift towards the door, their minds turning towards lunch. Their candlelit shadows were ash on the walls.

They were met at the Manor door by the housekeeper, wreathed in smiles.

'It's all over,' she blurted out, unable to contain herself. 'Mr. Kennedy and Mr. Khruschev, they spoke on the phone and the Russian ships have turned round.' For a moment, they all stood in the hall not knowing how to react, like prisoners who had suddenly found their cell doors unlocked. Then Alicia let out a joyful whoop which didn't sound like her at all, and the men began shaking hands as if it were they who had masterminded the telephone call. Ginny slipped away, unnoticed, to take Pip to Nanny, who would be waiting in the nursery to put him down for his nap.

She should have gone straight back down, but she lingered, watching quietly as Nanny changed Pip out of the christening gown and settled him to rest.

'You should go down, Mrs. Philip,' Nanny urged. 'He'll settle better once you've gone, and I expect they'll all be wanting lunch, don't you?' The suggestion of celebration hung in the air between them but neither made any mention of the news.

'In a minute, Nanny. You go to your lunch, I can settle him.' Nanny looked doubtful about this, but she had her instructions and she went. Ginny remained where she was, on the window seat, whose cushion was covered in a much -faded fabric depicting cowboys and Indians, where Philip used to read The Snow Queen. The ice was in her own heart now. She felt cheated. She could not endure lunch with her relieved and happy family because, though she was only now fully conscious of it, she had been relying on the missile crisis to erase her discontents. What now? She looked around at the nursery's faded comforts. The smell of roast beef insinuated itself into the room as it had, no doubt, for generations of Van Heppel Sundays. What now?

'You know, don't you?' she said to Pip, who was not asleep and turned his head towards the sound of her voice. She held his pale, unblinking gaze. 'You know it's alright for me to think like this because you were always going to live. I've done everything you needed me to. I could have gone…'

So much time all of a sudden, stretching out to infinity in front of her. So many years for Alicia and Bonn, to be paced out from the wedding portrait on the piano. So much time for Frank to serve.

And for herself?

She looked away, out towards the sea. The cloud had lifted since morning and the boundary between sea and sky was a charcoal smudge along the horizon, a line and its shadow. The Island was invisible from this angle but clear to her mind's eye, a solution known but not yet proven.

## Author's Note

Readers who are lucky enough to know the Suffolk coast-line will feel the shadow of Orford and its extraordinary history behind this book. While Orford inspired it, my seaside town of Aldeford and everything which happens in it is entirely fictional.

# Acknowledgements

A book has many midwives. I would like to thank, first and foremost, my editor and publisher Sam Ruddock, whose perceptive editing and faith in this book have helped to make it what it is. I would also like to thank my early readers: Kate Griffin, Fairless Masterman, Lucy Popp, Sara Werry, Katie Woods, Karen Vermuelen Grainger and Debbie Vince.

Thanks also to Joanne Reardon and Heather Richardson without whose wise and encouraging advice about another book entirely, this one probably wouldn't have been written.

Thanks to Suzie Hanna and Hayley Matthews for the inspiring conversations and the promise of dance, and to Al MacFarlane for creative companionship and encouragement.

We are lucky, in Norwich, to be the home of the National Centre for Writing which has supported me in many ways over many years. Thank you to Chris Gribble, Peggy Hughes and all the NCW team, and a special shout-out to Simon Jones, Alice Kent and Flo Reynolds who are no longer part of that team but very much part of my writing life. Freya Gallagher-Jones gets a thank you all of her own in acknowledgement of our shared years in the teeth of the Dragon.

With love to Guy, Mei, Hugh, Laurice, Kairo, Cassius and Rudi. My people.

# Thank you for supporting planet-positive publishing

Story Machine seeks to have a net positive social and environmental impact. That means the environment and people's lives are actually better off for every book we print. Story Machine offsets our entire carbon footprint plus 10% through a www.ClimateCare.org programme. We are now investing in converting to use only 100% renewable energies and seeking out the most planet-positive means of shipping books to our readers.

The printing industry is a huge polluter, requiring the use of huge amounts of water, toxic chemicals, and energy. Even FSC certified mix paper sources drive deforestation. That's why we are proud to be working with www.Seacort.net, a global leader in planet positive printing. Not only have they developed a waterless and chemical-free process, they use only 100% renewable energies, FSC certified recycled paper, and direct absolutely no waste to landfill. That's why they were crowned Europe's most sustainable SME in 2017, and have been recognised as one of the top three environmental printers in the world.

Planet-positive printing costs us a little more. But we think this is a small price to pay for a better world, today and in the future. If you agree, please share our message, and encourage other publishers and authors to commit to planet-positive printing. Stories can change the world. They deserve publishers that want to make sure they do.

Together, we can make publishing more sustainable.